THE DEVIL
WEARS WINGS

Also by Harry Whittington

A TICKET TO HELL
FORGIVE ME, KILLER
WEB OF MURDER

THE DEVIL WEARS WINGS

HARRY WHITTINGTON

Black Lizard Books

Berkeley • 1987

Black Lizard Books are distributed by Creative Arts Book
Company. For information contact: Black Lizard Books,
833 Bancroft Way, Berkeley, CA 94710.

Composition by QuadraType.

ISBN 0-88739-036-6
Library of Congress Catalog Card No. 86-71964

Manufactured in the United States of America.

I REMEMBER IT WELL

Harry Whittington

My writing life has been a blast. With all the fallout, fragmentation, frustration and free-falls known to man. I've careened around on heights I never dreamed of, and simmered in pits I wouldn't wish on my worst enemy, and survived. Maybe it's just that I forget quickly and forgive easily.

Looking back, I find it perhaps less than total extravaganza. It all seemed so great at the time: Doing what I wanted to do, living as I wanted to live, having the time of my life and being paid for it. I worked hard; nobody ever wrote and sold 150-odd novels in 20 years without working hard, but I loved what I was doing. I gave my level best on absolutely every piece of my published work, for one simple reason: I knew of no other way to sell what I wrote.

I've known some wonderful people in the writing racket. For some years, I lived in a loose-knit community of real, hard working writers—Day Keene, Gil Brewer, Bill Brannon, Talmage Powell, Robert Turner, Fred C. Davis. Out in Hollywood, Sid Fleischman and Mauri Grashin are friends, as were Fred C. Fox, Elwood Ullman. And via mail, Frank Gruber, Carl Hodges, Milt Ozaki. Death flailed that company of gallants—Gruber, Fox, Hodges, Ullman, Keene, Gil Brewer, Brannon, Fred Davis—all gone. Talmage Powell's inimitable stories appear in anthologies and magazines and, as of this writing, as I did in the wild and wonderful fifties when we all were young and pretty, I persist.

The fifties. The magic. Time of change. Crisis. The end of the pulps and the birth of the "original" paperbacks. In recent years critic-writers, Bill Pronzini, Christopher Geist, Michael Barson and Bill Crider have kindly referred to me as "king of the paperback pioneers." I didn't realize at the time I was a pioneer and I certainly didn't set out to be "king" of anything. I needed a fast-reporting, fast-paying market; the paperbacks provided this. I wrote eight, 10, 12 hours a day. Paperback editors bought and paid swiftly. We were good for each other.

The reason why I wrote and sold more than almost everybody else was that I was living on the edge of ruin, and I was naive.

James Cagney once said, "It's the naive people who become the true artists. First, they have to be naive enough to believe in themselves. Then, they must be naive enough to keep on trying, using their talent, in spite of any kind of discouragement or doublecross. Pay no attention to setbacks, not even know a setback when it smites. Money doesn't concern them."

Money concerned me. I'd never have dared become a full-time writer if I'd known in the forties that the critically acclaimed "authors" I admired from afar were college professors, ad men, lawyers, reporters, dogcatchers or politicians by day. Fewer than 500 people in the U.S. make their living from full-time free-lance writing. Since 1948, I've been precariously, one of fortune's 500. I persist.

Because, in 1948, I didn't know any better, I quit my government job of 16 years and leaped in, fully clothed, where only fools treaded water. I had a wife, two children and gimlet-eyed creditors standing at my shoulder. I had to write and I had to sell.

At that precise moment, the publishing world was being turned upside down by the Fawcett Publishing Company. When they lost a huge reprint paperback distribution client, they decided to do the unheard of, the insane. They published original novels at 25¢ a copy. Print order on each title: 250,000. They paid writers not by royalty but on print order. Foreign, movie and TV rights remained with the writer. They were insane. They were my kind of people. Bill Lengel, Dick Carroll and later, Walter Fultz. Elegant men. One hell of a publishing company.

Jim Quinn at HandiBooks; Graphic, Mauri Latzen of Star, and Avon were all swift-remitting markets once the spillgates broke open. I wrote and they bought. Once Sid

Fleischman wrote from Santa Monica: "Just came from the downtown newsstands. My God, Harry, you've taken them over."

It wasn't true. It just seemed true.

It wasn't all easy, not all beer and peanuts. There were rough times. You want dues paid?

I came to writing from a love of words. However, I wrote for at least 13 years before I truly learned to plot.

I admired extravagantly Scott Fitzgerald's writings all through the '30s when almost everyone else had forgotten him or, if they remembered, thought he had died, along with prosperity, in 1929. I couldn't afford to buy THE GREAT GATSBY, so I borrowed it over and over from the public library. I haunted used bookstores looking for old magazines in which Fitzgerald might appear.

I met a girl who bought for me—at one hell of an expense in the deepest Depression because they were out of print—all of Fitzgerald's books. I was so overcome with gratitude and joy and exultance that I married her. I still have her, and the books.

I spent at least seven years writing seriously and steadily before I sold anything. June 12, 1943, I sold a short-short story to United Features for $15. In the next couple years I sold them about 25 more 1000-worders, but it was five more years before I sold regularly. In that time, I worked for more than two years with a selfless, patient editor at Doubleday on a book they finally rejected. At this moment, Phoenix Press bought my first western novel, VENGEANCE VALLEY, July 10, 1946.

Using my navy GI bill, I studied writing. Suddenly the scales fell from my eyes. I understood plotting, emotional response, story structure. Fifteen years it took me to learn, but I knew. I could plot—forward, backwards, upside down. It was like being half-asleep and abruptly waking. Never again would I be stumped for plot idea or story line. From the moment I learned to plot, I was assaulted with ideas screaming, scratching and clawing for attention. For the next 20 years I sold everything I wrote. I enjoyed Cadillacs, Canoe cologne, cashmere, Hickey-Freeman jackets and charge accounts you would not believe.

I wrote suspense novels, contemporary romances, westerns, regional "backwoods" tales. People who wonder such things, wondered how I could crossover in these genres with such ease.

All very simple. I could write backwoods sagas because I came from mid-Florida when it was truly Kinnan-Rawlings territory. I could write "cattle-country" fiction because I lived in my teen years on a farm with cows. We had less than a hundred, but when you've known one cow, you've known a thousand. When you've hand-pumped ten-gallon tubs of water from 100-foot well to fill those bellies, you know more than you need to know. I spent time on horseback, usually without a saddle. When I fell, as I frequently did, unsecured and fast-moving, that wonderful horse stopped in midstride and stood silently until I crawled back aboard. I didn't need to know a thousand horses, I just needed to love that one.

I never wrote westerns about "cowboys" or indians or "hold-up men." I wrote about people in a raw rugged land who loved, hated, feared and saw murder for what it was—murder. They got sick at the thought of using a gun. They used guns as you would in the same situation—as a last resort.

There was much talk in the fifties about the writers who "lived" their suspense stories. I didn't write that kind of suspense story anyway. I wrote about *people*, their insides, their desires, and fears and hurts and joys of achievement and loss. I wrote about love which flared white hot and persisted against all odds, because I was fool enough then to believe—and I still believe—that true love does persist, does not alter when it alteration finds. It may buckle in the middle sometimes, but it does not bend with the remover to remove.

If a character hurt in his guts, I wrote to make you *feel* how bad he hurt. I knew about emotional pain, which is the worst kind, and about physical pain. I was in two fights. In one, I got my front teeth smashed loose. In the other, over-matched, I was struck sharply in each temple by fists with third knuckle raised like a knot. When I wrote about pain, I knew what I was talking about. You don't have to die in a fire to write truly about arson.

How I came to write suspense stories is something

else. Bill Brannon, in Chicago, said he could sell all the suspense novelettes—about 10,000 words each—I could write.

Since I wanted only to be Scott Fitzgerald, with a touch of sardonic Maugham and J.P. McEvoy humor, I told Bill I hated suspense stories, never read them, and certainly couldn't write them. But I was in Chicago attending a writers' conference when I said that.

Having no idea what hellish jokes fate had stored up for me, I caught the bus home from Chicago—36 hours of leaving the driving to them. I was hemmed in against a window by a lady who looked like a giant-economy sized Nell Carter. In an attempt to escape, my mind plotted out the first suspense story I'd ever attempted. I got home on a Monday, wrote the story that night and mailed it the next day to Bill. That Friday I got a check from King Features Syndicate for $250. For at least 20 years I got small royalty checks from King Features on the 30 novelettes I did for them starting in 1949.

My path had been chosen for me. Fredric Pohl, who was an agent then, sold my first western novelette to Mammoth Western, "Find This Man With Bullets." Bill Brannon sold my suspense novel, SLAY RIDE FOR A LADY to Jim Quinn at Handibooks. I was on my way. I was less than a household name, but I was too busy, and having too much fun, to care. The people who read my books said I was a good writer, a damned good writer. How could I argue with that?

The New York *Times*, July 18, 1954: "Whittington does the best sheer story telling since the greatest pre-sex days of the detective pulps . . . YOU'LL DIE NEXT is a very short novel, which is just as well. I couldn't have held my breath any longer in this vigorous pursuit tale whose *plot* is too dexteriously twisted even to mention in a review."

Baby, I could *plot!*

From *Ellery Queen Mystery Magazine* (Paris Edition) 1958: "MAN IN THE SHADOW—Whittington's style is uncommonly lean and bare—it must have been difficult for the adapter to get his tone for French readers. But the impact is vigorous, the craftsmanship so smooth that one identifies with these characters, in their anxieties, their furies, their indignation, their rebelling against injustice, so we fully recommend this book to you."

And *Le Monde*, the largest newspaper of Paris, 1957: "With this novel, FRENZIE PASTORALE (*Desire in the Dust*), which compares favorably with Erskine Caldwell's best, Whittington asserts himself as one of the greats among American novelists." You can imagine how I blushed.

Nov. 4, 1955, the New York *Times:* "In THE HUMMING BOX, Whittington once again proves himself one of the most versatile and satisfactory creators of contemporary fiction—tightly told, recalling the best of early James M. Cain."

"SADDLE THE STORM, is one of the top six westerns of this year" said the *Saturday Review of Literature*, and the Western Writers of America voted SADDLE THE STORM number one of the 10 best paperback westerns of 1954.

Fifteen of my novels sold to motion pictures. Three television series were based on my books.

I was living high. One of the few people doing exactly what I wanted to do. In 1957, Warner Brothers hired me to write a screenplay from my western novel TROUBLE RIDES TALL for Gary Cooper. I couldn't write an adaptation that excited them. Finally, my option was dropped, the project became LAWMAN, a TV series starring John Russell and Peter Brown which ran about five years.

I had contracted the movie virus in Hollywood. I returned to Florida, wrote, produced and directed—and could not sell to a distributor—a horror film called FACE OF THE PHANTOM.

For the next eight years I could not produce or sell enough scripts to stay ahead of howling creditors. My agent decided I must do only nonfiction—things like "How I Made a Million in Florida Real Estate"—though I knew or cared nothing about the subject. He rejected out of hand the next five novels I submitted, then when I sold them myself, he demanded his ten percent because the books had once been in his office. He even wrote letters to editors threatening to sue if they bought my work except through him. I went to court and six months later I was free of him. But I had to write true confessions under my wife's name in order to keep my son in college during the long fight.

I signed, in 1964, to do a 60,000-word novel a month for a publisher under his house names. I was paid $1000. On the first of each month. I wrote one of these novels a month for 39 months. At the same time I was Robert Hart Davis, doing several 30,000-word novels for *Man-from-Uncle Magazine*. Strange things happened at Gold Medal. Walter Fultz called with the great news that my novel DON'T SPEAK TO STRANGE GIRLS had at first reporting sold 85 percent and was certain for immediate reprintings. Instead, nothing happened and Fawcett, which had been since 1950 like family, suddenly rejected everything I submitted. Walter Fultz even wrote a nice letter apologizing. The next thing Fawcett published by me was the novelization FALL OF THE ROMAN EMPIRE for which I "was the only writer for the job."

DESERT STAKEOUT went into six printings For Gold Medal once they did business with me again. CHARRO was reprinted five times.

The novel a month with the other work I was trying to do, plus the tensions and the debts, exhausted me. Emotionally. Mentally. Physically. I cried at weather reports. Then came the *coup de grace*. My new agent got me an assignment to do an original novel using the characters from the TV series MAN FROM UNCLE. The publisher had issued 30 of my novels and said he'd done well indeed. I'd always had royalty contracts from him. Now he wanted to pay $1500 for outright purchase of all rights.

What in hell had happened to me? Wasn't I the same writer who'd been giving the best he knew for 20 years? The agent advised me to accept. But he and the publisher knew what I didn't know. Mike Avallone had written the first *Man From Uncle* novel. It had sold at least a million copies and Mike was bleeding in rage.

So now it was my turn. I signed the contract. I wrote the book. I saw it on the Chicago *Tribune* paperback best seller list for *one full year* and I, who owed my shirt, made $1500 on a book that would easily have paid off all I owed and more.

I wanted to go on, pay no attention to setbacks, overlook discouragement or doublecross. With all my heart I wanted to, but I was too tired, too disappointed, too depleted.

So, sadly, I closed up shop. I still loved to write, but nobody cared, nobody wanted me. I figured if I were less than nothing to one of my most consistent publishers, I had come to a low place indeed. I had come by winding roads to the place where an agent and publisher conspired to use me for money the IRS wouldn't let them keep anyway.

I threw away every unsold script, put my books in storage. I quit. I asked for a job as an editor in the US Dept. of Agriculture, and they hired me for Rural Electrification Administration.

I had reached the low place where writing lost its delight, the place where I refused to go on. No working writer knew more about plotting than I. Fifteen years it took me to learn. Twenty years I practiced. I was a damn good writer. I knew what made a scene real, what made a heart break or a reader respond. But I also knew nobody gave a damn.

For seven years, I worked in the government. I did sell three books in seven years because I felt *guilty* when I wasn't at my typewriter. What else was I? What else did I know?

In 1974, my wife—that same girl who bought out-of-print Scott Fitzgerald for me in 1935—got the name and address of literary agent Anita Diamant. Want a plot gimmick? She got Anita's address from Bill Brannon who'd sold my first suspense stories in 1947.

Mrs. Diamant arranged for me to become Ashley Carter. Since 1975, I've written the Falconhurst and Blackoaks novels, the antebellum slave stories of the Mandingo slaves done by Kyle Onstott and then Lance Horner.

Then I learned that during those seven years of exile, I hadn't been totally forgotten. Jean-Jacques Schleret, a French critic of Strasbourg, wrote to my Hollywood agent, Mauri Grashin, to learn when Whittington had died since there had been no Whittington suspense novel in France since 1968.

The *Magazine Literaire* (Paris) wrote: "For the past 25 years, we in France have considered Whittington one of the masters of the *romain noir* in the second generation—after Hammett, Chandler, Cain of the first generation . . . his novel BRUTE IN BRASS is one of the finest of the genre ever written. . . ."

Gallimard, which had published my books in *Séqrie Noire* now was reprinting them in *Carre Noir*. The french equivalent of the Mystery Writers of America, 813, Les Amis Du Crime, published a book devoted to my work.

The 813 and the Maison d'Andre Malraux invited Kathryn and me as Guest of Honor at the Fourth Festival of Suspense Novels and Films at Reims in Oct. 1982. Along with Evan Hunter, I was the first American writer to be invited to join 813. I was treated with such kindness and love and awe and attention that the entire celebration seems more dream than reality.

It was all an elegant and brilliant party. The French were the kindest hosts on earth. Jean-Jacques Schleret, Jean Paul Schweighaeuser, Rafael Sorin, Stephane Bourgoin, Francois Gerif and Robert Louit, all wrote glowingly of my work.

Back home in America Bill Crider, Bill Pronzini, Michael Barson and others praised my old suspense and western novels.

I wasn't dead after all.

This spontaneous outpouring of affection and warmth in France and here at home restored my old lost excitement and enthusiasms. It was like plodding for a long time in lonely night wind and coming suddenly upon a bright and festive place loud with love and laughter.

Rafael Sorin, writing in *Le Monde*, Paris: "(Whittington) . . . this prolific writer of more than 140 novels is largely unappreciated. He holds, nevertheless, an honorable position among that intermediate generation of the American suspense novel alongside David Goodis, Don Tracy and Wm. Campbell Gault. Even the most minor of Whittington's earliest narratives reread today does not fail to charm. Whittington, who acknowledges the influences of Cain, Fredric Davis and Day Keene is the most violent writer of this genre. His tomb of death can be the appliance freezer, alligators, mosquitoes carrying fatal virus. But his worst enemy is *la femme*. She who kills for money and devours those who succumb to her charms. . . . Whittington, who appeared pictured in his early books to be a rebellious young turk, arrives at Reims looking like a casting director's dream-ideal of the well-fed, successful TV lawyer. . . ."

The *West Coast Review of Books* in 1979 awarded Porgys to my RAMPAGE as "best contemporary novel" and PANAMA as "best historical novel based on fact." WHO'S WHO IN AMERICA decided to include me in their august pages. *Twentieth Century Crime & Suspense Writers* were most flattering as was *Twentieth Century Western Writers*.

Aroused by affection to optimism and resolution again, I could even remember the good which had accrued in the worst of times: The night at the Mystery Writers Award Dinner when I was introduced to Howard Browne, then executive editor at Mammoth Western. Howard greeted me, "My God, I'm glad to meet you. My chief editor Lila Shaffer says you're the most exciting new writer she's read. Better get a lot of material in to her fast. You've got a real fan there."

Or Harry Stephen Keeler, in his 80s and still selling his convoluted mysteries, writing in those years when sex in books was two passionate sighs, two loosened buttons and three asterisks: "Whittington is the only writer I know who can make a sex scene last for six pages without ever going out of bounds."

Or that most caring and selfless lady literary agent of Copenhagen who wrote, deeply troubled, in the midst of my 1960 battle to be free of an agent who admittedly planned to destroy me: "I cannot believe this man would risk losing your great talent for writing by his insensitive and selfish behavior. I have taken the liberty of writing to five New York agents (names and addresses enclosed) who each promise me they would welcome you, with sensitivity, caring and support, as a client."

It's been a wonderful life and I've met some wonderful people; it's been one hell of a roller-coaster ride.

Scott Fitzgerald once wrote: "There are no second acts in America." Maybe he was right. Maybe not. Maybe the trick is to hang in there—until after the intermission.

And, before we part, a few words about this book before you and the others selected for this classic-suspense-novel revival that constitutes the Black Lizard series.

Questions most often asked: Why did you write a particular novel, how long did it take to write it, where'd you get the idea for it and, where do you get your ideas?

First, my story germs are contracted differently than those of some of the leading practitioners of suspense and mystery, and even western, writing. Several stellar-performer-writers have averred on TV and other public dais that they start to write with no idea where they're going, or how their tale will resolve itself. One famous gentleman, writing for beginning writers, said he rewrote the ending of one book several times before making it come out right.

Despite the protestations of these best-selling writers, I personally find this lack of planning wasteful, unprofessional, and worst, even amateurish. Sometimes, I realize it's said to sound artistic. Still, it's much like setting out in a billion-dollar shuttle for outer space with no flight plan. Head for the moon, but if you land on Mars, what the hell? It's like a magician's walking on stage without knowing if he will draw rabbit or dove or anything at all out of his hat. In my world of writing at least, suspense is for the reader, not the writer. I can't believe bridges are built without minute preparations, or that Donald Trump okays a new tower which might turn out to look like the World Trade Center or Mr. Toad's Wild Ride at Disney World.

I usually start at the crisis, climax or dramatic denouement of my story, even if it's sparked by some unusual scene, character, situation or speculation. A story is not about "an innocent man framed by his own government" but how—with what special, carefully foreshadowed strength, skill, knowledge or character trait—he overcomes this terrifying situation. That "planting" and a preconceived "emotional effect" which will gratify, shock and involve the reader is truly what the novel is all about. Or, as Mickey Spillane said, "The first page sells the book being read, the last page sells the one you're writing."

Once a writer sets in his own mind "how" a story-line will be resolved, he is then freed to torment, tease, terrify or tantalize his audience. Alfred Hitchcock called this story core "the McGuffin," Harry Cohn of Columbia Pictures called it the "wiener." I call it the key, the complication factor, the gimmick.

Don't take my word for it. Let me quote Edgar Allan Poe who wrote, in reviewing Nathaniel Hawthorne's *Twice Told Tales:* "A skillful artist has constructed a tale. If wise, he has not fashioned his thoughts to accommodate his incidents but, having conceived, with deliberate care, a certain unique or SINGLE EFFECT (caps mine) to be brought out, he *then* (italics mine) invents such incidents, he then combines such effects as may best aid him in establishing this *preconceived* effect. If his initial sentence tend not to the outbringing of this effect, then he has failed in his first step. In the whole composition there should be no word written of which the tendency, direct or indirect, is not in the pre-established design. And by such means, and with such care and skill, a picture is at length painted which leaves in the mind of him who contemplates it with a kindred art, a sense of the fullest satisfaction. The idea of the tale has been presented unblemished, because undisturbed. . . ."

And I believe a good cabinet-maker can build a cabinet without rebuilding it forty-seven times. And I suggest he likely lays out his entire plan before he starts to build.

Having said this, I immediately stipulate that some of these writers who embark boldly with only nebulous idea, dramatic first scene or unusual character, have sold more books than Poe and I combined (and including Nathaniel Hawthorne). I still hold to my battered barricades. I still don't want to put myself in the untenable position where, when all else fails, I must resort to God in the machinery or "come to realize."

Anyhow, once I have worked out a "plot key" which will unlock my mystery, I know where I am going, even if I don't know how I will get there. I wish I could illustrate with examples of "plot keys" from these present novels without destroying your pleasure in them in advance, but I am sure you will discover them for yourself and, best of all, you won't be abandoned with the sense that the "outcome" was thrown in from left field. The climax will be carefully planted and foreshadowed, which is simply a matter of sweat and blood and hard work called "plotting."

French critics have noted that my heroes all are "disillusioned knights in rusted armor, often at battle with the very forces which employed them in the first place." I had no idea, as I wrote, that this was true, but in the face of so much evidence, I must concede. No one of my heroes is ever permitted, by his own disenchanted sanity, to believe in the sanity of the social "order" around him. For example, a nation in which an administration bases its policy on industrial/military complex greed, can talk blandly the insanity of "winning a nuclear war," insists upon sixteen thousand atomic warheads when three will be more than sufficient, and spend billions on it while refusing crumbs to dependent children and closing the Library of Congress at 5 P.M. daily; perhaps because that leadership got where it is by having never read more than three books in its combined life span, and wishing to provide every youth that same opportunity. My hero cannot put on the happy face. He is pushed to the place where he can trust only himself, even when he recognizes the impossible odds he faces. This does not stop him because he would rather die fighting than to surrender to greed, corruption and meanheartedness, which places him as often at war with himself as with the uncompassionate and cynical power structure.

I often quoted FORGIVE ME, KILLER as answer to those who wanted to know how long it took me to write one of my suspense novels—and what delayed me?

With FORGIVE ME, KILLER, the answer is either four years or one month. I make no attempt to resolve the question, I simply state the facts: On March 8, 1952, I signed a contract with Fawcett Gold Medal for a novel (in outline) called MY BLOODY HANDS. Nothing went right. It was planned as a novel about a crooked cop named Mike Ballard who is gut-sick of corruption and his own smell of evil. He tries to atone for and redress the wrongs of his rotten city. But, as I wrote, I and Bill Lengel and Richard Carroll at Gold Medal saw it lacked something. One knew from the outset what the end would be. They had paid me a $1000 advance which they told me to keep and to get to work on something else.

By 1956, I was still stewing over that Mike Ballard novel and getting no answers. I accompanied a friend to a prison to interview an inmate for a *True Detective* article. When we arrived in late afternoon, we walked through a vaguely illumined, vast tomb-like auditorium where, far down front, the prison orchestra was rehearsing.

With this strange, eerie picture in mind, everything suddenly fell into place for the long abandoned novel: its mood, tempo, structure, complication gimmick, everything. Mike Ballard was no longer a disgusted cop but a man on the take and content with status quo. Don't ask me why, because I don't know, but when I returned home, I started anew and in about a month had finished the Mike Ballard novel. I now called it HELL CAN'T WAIT, Gold Medal called it BRUTE IN BRASS, the French publisher Gallimard called it VINGT-DEUX and many French critics called it "one of the best of the *romain noir* genre ever written."

Did I write FORGIVE ME, KILLER in four weeks, or did it take four long years? Whatever, I hope you find it intriguing.

FIRES THAT DESTROY was written to the classic mold of "character proof." (Becky Sharp's selfish ambition in VANITY FAIR is the best example). You establish your character with a strong (even obsessive) character trait and then prove that trait when in a crisis the character has the opportunity to be something more or less than the inner drive prodding him. When he behaves "in character" no matter the cost, his trait has been proved. I am betraying no secrets when I tell you my protagonist, Bernice, wanted above everything else to be regarded with the esteem and respect shown the loveliest of women. How she is given that attention and proves her trait is the story of this novel.

The hero—and he is one of my few truly unblemished heroes—in TICKET TO HELL is indeed the battered knight tilting against terrible odds and for no promise of reward. This does not stop him from fighting for what he wants—a truly disenchanted knight in rusted armor with only what he is inside, and an old long-lost love he cannot recover, to sustain him.

WEB OF MURDER, on the other hand, is one of those sweetly plotted novels Day Keene, Fred Davis and James

Cain used to concoct. We start the protagonist almost casually down the road to Hades and then follow him on every cruel twist and turn through increasing terror to the pit beyond hell. The reviewer who said WEB OF MURDER "proves that the death penalty may not be the worst punishment" exactly expressed the key to this novel. If you have half the fun reading it that I had writing it, we've got something going here.

The events in THE DEVIL WEARS WINGS are totally true and documented. This botched, bourbon-laced crime was one I wrote for editor Joe Corona at Fawcett's *True Detective*. But I could not get this tragic-comedy out of my mind, so I structured the true events enough to give them form, a beginning, middle, end and desired emotional effect.

The novel here titled A MOMENT TO PREY had a history almost as varied as its titles. When I wrote it, I called it NEVER FIND SANCTUARY, which Gold Medal changed to BACKWOODS TRAMP and which the publisher Gallimard, of Paris, called LE CHANT D'ALLIGATOR. It is one of my favorites. But I suppose a writer is like a proud parent: among his children he has none but favorites.

August 1986

Chapter One

They gave me the okay from the control tower and I told the girl to take it down. I had been telling her she was going to be all right, and sometimes it looked as if she'd make it, but now I knew better. I had been upstairs with her for about an hour and this was more than enough. I needed a drink, I needed to lie down somewhere until the knots in my stomach loosened; what I really needed was to vomit. She sank the stabilizer, but pulled back too far and I tried to keep my voice level as I warned her to take it easy. When I spoke, she went to sweat and rode the brake. The tires struck concrete, squealing. We hopped straight up about twenty feet and I didn't say anything. But when the Cessna's right wing-tip scorched the runway, that's when I really yelled.

I put my lungs and my guts into it. That yell had been stacking up in me for a long time and when I finally unfroze her and took the controls and taxied along the chute toward the hangar, the woman, the plane and I were still trembling.

I cut the engine, killing it in the shadow of the damnedest sign I ever saw. It compounded the illness in me every time I brought in a plane, walked toward it, or remembered it over a beer. Sunpark International Airport is a sprawling flat with take-off patterns that accommodate the new jet service ships. It is a way station between Miami, New Orleans, Havana, South America, New York. Huge metal cribs house Eastern, Delta, American, Pan-Am, ASA. All the big lines touch down there, but as far as I was concerned that sign, sprawled across the entrance of Hangar 2, dwarfed and mocked everything else on the field.

"Smiling Jimmy Clark Can Teach *You* to Fly." Jimmy Clark's smiling face covered the whole left end of the sign, and his face was bigger than his plane. I always mistrust a man who eternally smiles, and he had the kind of smile that

1

made my skin crawl. His thick red hair was like a tight skull cap over a short forehead and squinted blue eyes you still couldn't see into even when his photo was blown up bigger than his own estimation of himself.

One thing you had to admit about that picture. It was a perfect likeness. The only lie was the sign itself. Jimmy Clark couldn't teach you to fly. He'd been piloting planes for twenty-five years and still was no flier. Jimmy Clark could smile, though. His photo proved this.

My pupil got out of the Cessna first, still shaken, and very pale. "I guess I washed out," she said.

I jumped out on the grease-spotted cement beside her. I was aware of a dozen things at once: grease jockeys grinning in a knot inside the shadowed hangar, watching us but pretending they weren't; the pattern of black sky-chutes in geometric lines dictated by the wind's will; the neon passenger-service signs glowing palely in the stark white sunlight; Jimmy Clark standing in the doorway of his glass-partitioned office and not smiling; the look of illness in the girl's face. But mostly I was thinking my legs felt as though I'd finally reached shore after wading a long time in a rough surf.

"I washed out. I really washed out," she said. I glanced at her and that's when I realized she was bearing down too hard on it. She wanted me to lie to her. She wasn't upset because of her miserable exhibition of flying; she was disturbed because I'd wailed at her like a dying weasel. She didn't want the truth at all.

I watched a fly crawl across the breast of her flying jacket. She'd bought expensive, fashionable flying togs.

I felt myself tightening up again. I hadn't disliked her before, but suddenly I saw her as she really was, and it was everything I'd lived to hate in a female. She had this chopped hair and a full-fed face and flat eyes you can't see into and a superior air that was bred into her from the day she was born expecting everything handed to her and getting it. She was full in the face, full in the breasts, full in the hips because she'd been fed and pampered and spoiled until she was soft everywhere except in her attitude toward other people, women who crossed her and men who didn't snap to heel.

2

I pulled my gaze up to her face. She was slightly taller than I, because let's face it, the only place I'm a big man is behind the controls of a plane. I touch five-seven, standing on the ground. I find myself looking up to most guys, and some women. Nobody ever hated standing on the ground more than I did once I learned to fly.

"I'm no damn good. I'm never going to learn, Buz."

I licked my tongue around the inside of my mouth. It felt cottony dry. I needed a drink and couldn't help looking toward the Rudder upstairs in the clean-lined, blue-metal-and-glass administration building. The kindliest thing I could think to tell her at the moment was that even some birds aren't equipped to fly. But I wasn't feeling very kindly.

"Are you mad with me, Buz?"

"Why should I be mad?" I couldn't help it if my voice shook slightly.

"You are mad. I don't blame you. I almost wrecked the plane, almost killed both of us."

I squinted against the sun. "I've been nearer dead plenty of times."

"But not because of stupidity."

"You got a point there."

She caught her breath, drew herself up and I saw the resentment and anger in her eyes. I could also see the college she attended, the sorority she ruled. She could say what she liked about herself; it was all clever and joking anyhow. But me she had paid some money. She had paid me to lie to her, to make her look as good as those tailored togs.

The fly got tired and flew away. The fly was lucky.

"You could be a little nice about it." Her mouth got sulky.

I could feel the trembling start in my stomach. I could be nice to her, help her get a license, invite her to take off and kill herself and any innocent bystanders. I wanted to give it to her straight. As far as I could see, a woman driving a car was bad enough, but a woman at the controls of a plane just didn't make pretty good sense. I was even willing to admit this was just one man's opinion. All I wanted was to tell her the truth.

I glanced across her shoulder and saw Jimmy Clark poised to smile in his office doorway.

3

He didn't have to say it: Who did I think I was? The C.A.A.? God? Did I think I owned this flying school? If I chased away paying customers, who would buy my beer?

"We all get nervous," I said.

"Yes." She was mollified. "I just got nervous. I don't know what was the matter. The earth was rushing up at me. It scared hell out of me. I know better."

"Sure you do. Buz Johnson's your teacher. You got to know better."

"What went wrong, Buz?"

I wanted to hit her. My fist was a soggy doughnut at the end of my arm. I wanted to tell her what went wrong: You got up this morning, doll. You put on those fancy togs and you drove out here, that's what went wrong.

Aloud, I said, "You got to take it easier. A big healthy doll like you. You got muscles. We'll talk about it tomorrow. Okay?"

She felt better; she forgave me. She squeezed my arm and walked away. I watched it for a while.

She could walk all right.

After a minute, Clark whistled me to heel. I turned around, feeling the sun bite into my shoulders, and walked into the hangar toward him. I wanted to get in out of the heat anyway.

Besides, where I was standing, I could still see that sign.

Chapter Two

As I moved out of the sun into the shade, I noticed this guy for the first time. He looked like something somebody had discarded and was still slumped where they'd left him. People are always standing around airfields, leaning against something, watching the planes, getting in the way, counting their money, and I wouldn't have given this character a thought except for the prickly sense I got that he was watching me and had been standing there for a long time reading me.

His face pulled into something resembling a smile and I saw he was going to speak to me. I shrugged out of my

4

jacket and walked on by him. When he saw I wasn't going to look at him he slumped back against the upright, not offended or worried, a man with plenty of time.

He looked most like an outsized rag doll that has been left out in the rain. He was over six feet tall but so thin he could have modeled CARE ads. His unruly hair looked as if it had been bleached and he kept jerking his head trying to keep a shag of it off his forehead. His face was lean, shadowed and hollow at the cheekbones with a pointed chin, but the thing you noticed most about him was the pouting of his mouth, as if the world never gave him a fair shake and he no longer expected it, and thick eyebrows even whiter than his hair.

"Mr. Johnson . . ."

He let his voice trail after me but I walked away from it. Jimmy Clark straightened in his doorway, a man with a slight potbelly, well-made suits in tasteless shades. He was the kind of man who is always telling you he ought to write the story of his life because he had really lived—married twice, flown mail, passengers and freight, and known everybody in flying worth knowing from Rick right on down. He hated planes and always had. They gave him a sick and queasy feeling when the motors turned over, and all he wanted now was to make a living and keep both feet on the ground. But as little as he knew about flying, it was all he knew. He'd accidentally gotten tangled up in it when he decided it was glamorous after seeing Buddy Rogers in "Wings," and he'd lived with his secret fright and gastric ulcers until he no longer knew how to breathe without them.

I walked toward him, thinking that he and I had each other, and maybe that was what we deserved. Whatever I'd had, I'd thrown away, using both hands if I couldn't throw it fast enough, and the truth was nobody would hire me any more except Jimmy Clark; no one, that is, with influence enough to keep my pilot's license. Jimmy Clark knew everybody and smiled at them. He sucked around, and he had a fair amount of influence, or perhaps an unfair amount. He stayed in business with his school, and he kept me licensed to fly. I suppose you might ask why I'd stay in Sunpark, if I hated it and hated Jimmy Clark and what I smilingly called my existence. Why this town, why this burg, why this particular hell? Did I think this hell preferable to any other? The answer was simple. It was the end of the line for me. I never consciously admitted this, or seldom admitted it, but down deep I knew it was true.

Clark's shirt collar was open, his tie was pulled awry, and it was difficult for him to smile. His armpits were sweaty and sweat beaded his upper lip.

"You trying to wreck my plane?"

"I could do that without trying."

"You gave it the old try out there. My God."

"You sign the pupils, pappy. I just fly the planes."

"She almost wrecked it, for God's sake."

"You don't have to brief me. I was riding with her."

"Don't you teach them anything? Don't you tell them anything? What do you do, just take them up in the air and sleep off your hangover?"

I walked by him, leaned against his desk.

"She's had the hours by now, Jim. If she was ever going to learn, she'd know by now."

Jimmy Clark smiled. You had to know him well to know how phony that smile was. "She's got plenty of money. She don't mind spending it, I don't mind taking it. She can take all the time she needs learning to fly. Is that clear, Ace?"

"Sure."

"I pay you to teach them."

I shrugged. "Some people just never can learn to fly. You ought to know that, Jimmy."

This wiped off the smile. "You bastard drunk. I was flying planes when you were a snot-nose."

I laughed at him. "Her excuse is she just hasn't learned yet, pappy. What's yours?"

His sweated face twisted into a smiling snarl. "Big war ace."

I shrugged again. "You take her up tomorrow."

He laughed. "What's with you, Ace? You come into money, talking to me like this?"

"No." I straightened up. "You don't like the way I teach the doll, you teach her."

I turned to walk away.

"Where you going?"

"What do you care?"

He stepped forward, caught my shoulder and put muscle in it. He pulled me around.

He was smiling.

"Take your hands off me, Clark." I could feel the shaking start in my hands.

"Don't walk away when I'm talking to you. I'll tell you when I'm through talking to you." His voice quavered. But he was still smiling.

"So talk."

"I might have something for you to do around here."

"I'll be back."

"I told you. I don't want you drinking on the job."

For no good reason, I remembered suddenly the way it had been when I first came back here to Sunpark after the Korean scrap. Clark had been impressed all to hell by my war record and my medals. He was the man who knew everybody worth knowing in aviation, and in those days he considered me one of the big ones. Maybe that was what gave him such a charge to push my face down in it when he paid me sixty bucks a week as a flying instructor.

I wiped the back of my hands across my mouth. My hands quivered just enough so I was too damned aware of it. God knew this was the point of no return. If I didn't tell him now where to go, I was going to have to buy an electric razor. I couldn't go on looking at myself in a shaving mirror mornings.

"Don't push it, Clark."

His smile pulled wider. He had me where he wanted me now, down where he wanted me. I could threaten to quit, and he could let me, he could fire me, at the top of his voice so it echoed to the rafters, and then I could beg him to take me back. Last stop. End of the line.

He waited, but when I didn't say anything, he became very polite. "I just wanted to ask you something, Buz."

I waited, feeling the weight of my jacket across my shoulder, feeling the quavering in my stomach that was never going to quiet, feeling those squinted eyes laughing at me, begging me to make trouble.

"Yeah?"

"This pupil. She say anything? She coming back tomorrow?"

I nodded. "She'll be here. Unless she gets killed crossing a street somewhere."

I waited another moment. He went on smiling but didn't say anything. I swallowed back the green sickness and walked away from him into the sunlight. I wasn't ever going to tell him where to go. And the real horror of this was, only one man knew this better than I did—smiling Jimmy Clark himself.

Chapter Three

This tall thin guy pulled himself away from the upright and shambled along, falling in step beside me. He even walked in a loose, rag-doll way, and I kept waiting for the stuffing to start dribbling out of his shirt sleeves.

"Mr. Johnson . . ."

He looked as if he intended walking along with me. I stopped, looking him over irritably. At the moment it didn't matter where he was headed. I wasn't going that way.

His bleached eyebrows wriggled like albino caterpillars.

"You had a close miss out there." He smiled, showing his front teeth.

"It happens."

"Don't know if I could take it."

"You a pilot?"

"No. Not exactly. Mr. Johnson, my name is Coates. Sid Coates."

I waited, looking at him without really seeing him. Maybe he was a prospective student. It would make Jimmy Clark unhappy if I discouraged him.

"You give flying lessons?" he said.

I jerked my head toward Clark's cubicle office inside the hangar. "See Jimmy Clark. He signs them on."

He bent forward slightly, smiling in a chummy, out-of-balance way. "Well, that's it. You see, I know something about planes. But I may not be any good, you see? Oh, I can do better now than that dame. But I always believed that flying was like playing the piano—I play the piano a little, too. What I mean is, a guy can play at the piano, and never

8

be any good. It's like that with being a pilot. You see what I mean?"

I nodded.

"And I figured, I don't want to mess around with it. If you knew me, you'd know I've messed around with a lot of things. Never did any good. I don't want to do that with flying. If I got it—fine. If I haven't I'll take up finger painting."

"You think I can look at you and tell?"

He smiled and those white eyebrows wriggled.

"No. I figured, you take me up for a short run. I expect to pay. But I'd trust your judgment. I've heard a lot about you, Mr. Johnson. You're the only man I'd take his word on a thing like this, just like that. I got a lot of respect for your opinion."

We leveled out above the town, and this far in the clean clear air above Jimmy Clark's sign, the tensions relaxed and I felt better. From three thousand feet the Florida country-side looked orderly, a simple geometric pattern of faded greens, brown, tan, a patch of plowed earth, each segment cut off and set apart squarely and cleanly. But even now I knew it wasn't so. The instant you touched ground again you knew better.

I talked mechanically, explaining the panel, the instruments. But Coates wasn't grabbing it. He was bored. He looked as if he had to bite his lip to keep from explaining this panel to me. I saw he'd lied. He knew more about a plane than he'd admitted down in the hangar. I got that uncomfortable feeling of wrong again, unexplained wrong, the kind that doesn't make any sense, but won't let you alone either.

"You want to handle her?" I said.

"You think it'll be all right?"

This feeling of wrong bugged me now, loud and clear. This boy was laying this respect for the war-hero flier pretty thick. He was giving me the old back rub. For some reason he was giving me the business, trying to make me purr.

"I don't know," I said. "We can't tell until you try it. Don't worry. We got dual controls and I got fast reactions."

He bestowed upon me another smile full of admiration

9

and I mistrusted him more than ever. It occurred to me that this boy was one of those—he could fly without a plane.

He took the controls and I gave him some simple commands. He executed them all well enough but in an awkward, rusty manner. It was obvious he'd had flight training, maybe a long time ago, but hadn't put in much flying time.

I taxied the Cessna back under Jimmy Clark's sign and Coates and I hit the cement. Clark was waiting in his office doorway wearing his smile like a cash register.

Coates thanked me and went inside the hangar to pay Clark. I watched his loose-gaited shuffle a moment but didn't wait for him. There wasn't anything more I could tell him. Sometime, somewhere he'd begun flight training, dropped it. He could resume it again, or not, that was his own decision to make.

I was thirsty.

I heard the pound of his shoes on the cement behind me. He was running in the sun to overtake me. I paused beside a chain-link fence outside Eastern's loading ramp. Men in coveralls and baseball caps were loading small trailers with suitcases and packages. On the runway a DC-7 was warming up, a pilot shouting out his window to the men on the ground below him. He was pointing to something on the right wing. For an instant, without meaning to at all, I listened to the revving engines. They sounded like Swiss clock movement. I glanced over my shoulder, putting all that out of my mind. Coates was breathing through his mouth when he came alongside.

"Buy you a drink, Buz?"

I looked him over, trying to find something in his pout-lipped face. There was nothing but the lopsided smile. But at least he'd dropped this business about wanting to be a flier, the kind of flier a man like Buz Johnson would admire. Here was a boy with a gimmick. I saw he wanted something.

I don't usually reject any offers of drinks, but I didn't want what went with this boy's offer.

"I don't think so," I said.

He grinned, wriggling his brows. "What's the matter, Buz? You don't drink?"

The way he said this I knew he'd learned plenty about me, and nobody ever learned anything about Buz Johnson without hearing early about his bar time.

It angered me. Whatever I was, it was my business.

"What do you want, Coates?"

He gave me that other-world smile and the flat eyes.

"Do I have to want something?"

"You don't have to. But you do."

He grinned. "Smart man."

"Forget it. I haven't got any."

"How do you know until we talk it over?"

"Maybe I'm tired. But so long." I walked away from him. He hesitated less than a second and then strode after me, his stilt-like legs working like scissor blades.

"Come on, Buz." He sounded exasperated. "We can have a drink together."

"Why?"

"Any law against it?"

"I don't know. Depends on what you want."

"My God. I like you. I want to be friendly."

People brushed by us on both sides, hurrying toward the loading gate. I watched my shortened shadow for a moment. I didn't try to keep the impatience out of my voice.

"You a lipso?"

"A what?"

"A pansy. A diver. A queer."

"My God." He laughed. "What makes you think that?"

"I don't know. You're something. You want something."

He nodded and we moved forward again, going against the current of chattering hurrying people. The p.a. system crackled out its last call for this flight. "Yes. I want something. But I'm not on the make for you." His laugh had an off-key sound. "Not this week. This week, everything is girls with me."

"So what you want?"

"Got a deal to discuss with you."

I stopped walking a few feet outside the glass doors of the administration building. The sun was hot against my head. I squinted slightly against the glare.

"A deal?"

"Might be a job for you."

"What kind of job?"

"You care? You need a good job, don't you?"

"Scram."

"You fool nobody." He stopped smiling, gave me a condescending pout. "Teaching dames to wreck planes. Taking lip from a jerk like that guy back there."

"I do all right."

"All right? Beer money. This is big. A real job."

"Doing what?"

"Flying. That's your racket, ain't it?"

I exhaled slowly. "This deal. Is it crooked?"

He shrugged. His brows moved as if they were laughing all by themselves at how naive one guy could get. Then he laughed, throwing it away. "What else?"

I turned and walked away from him.

I pushed open one of the glass doors. It felt chill against my hand, and the air conditioning cooled my face as I went through.

He ran after me. People glanced up from their leather chairs in the waiting area.

"Wait a minute. Don't get so holy."

"Get lost, Coates."

"I told you. This isn't just some crooked deal. It's big."

"I heard you."

"We can talk about it, can't we?"

"I'm a drunk," I said. "Not a thief."

I walked away from him again. This time I meant it and he didn't follow me. But when I was three or four steps away from him, he laughed.

"Not everybody is a drunk," he said after me. "But we're all thieves."

Chapter Four

I felt better after I'd had a whisky-and-beer in the Rudder. Only two things lifted me up any more: a good plane or a couple of drinks.

I sat on this stool, leaning on the bar, liking the looks and feel of this place, liking everything about it except the reflection of myself I kept bumping into when I stared straight ahead into the shadowy mirror. Even the shadowyness couldn't hide from me what I was. Forget it, boy, I told myself, maybe you aren't licked yet.

Maybe I wasn't licked, but I wasn't a boy any more, either. I still wanted the things I had wanted ten years ago and fifteen years ago. I had changed, but the things I wanted hadn't and were still as far removed as ever.

"How's it going, Buz?" the bartender said. He had close-cropped brown hair, close-shaved, round, chubby face, a neat white jacket. He complemented the vaguely lighted, swankly appointed Rudder Room. That was what I liked about this place, the quiet atmosphere of elegance. I hated hot, sweaty joints. This was the sort of drinking spot I wished I could afford.

I shrugged, motioned for a refill.

"Hear your pupil almost planted you this morning."

News travels fast around an airfield. I nodded. "She acted like she was mad at me."

"Somebody says she's not too large in the learning."

"She might make it, but it's going to be hard for her. Like impossible."

"Some social dame, isn't she?"

"Oh, she'll have a swank funeral." I lifted my glass. "I drink to her."

"Maybe you could teach her something else, Buz."

"Not me. Those rich dames—"

Somebody sat on the stool beside me. I was the only one at the bar at ten in the morning; the bar was lined with empty stools. I didn't have to look to see who it was.

"You mind?" Coates said.

"It's a public bar."

"Yeah. That's the way I figured it."

"I see you also waited until I'd had two drinks. You just don't know my capacity." I glanced up at the bartender. "Ollie, tell him about my capacity."

"In quarts or litres?" Ollie said.

"It's not like that at all," Coates said. "You see, I got to thinking. I mean—what we were talking about. I wanted to come in and ask you to forget it."

13

"So okay."

"Fine. I mean, hell, you're not interested. I mean, I'd appreciate it if you didn't mention what I said to anybody."

I didn't bother answering that.

He finished off a martini, sat twisting the glass stem in his fingers. His hands were thin and white with knobby knuckles. I didn't know what this boy had accumulated, but whatever it was, he'd never worked for it. His fingers and palms were hospital-white and uncalloused.

He said, "It was just that—well, I'd heard so much about you. You've got a war record a yard long. I mean, I really have heard about you. I mean even that freight airline you ran after the war."

I stared at the wet place on the bar, thinking about that freight line. We got hard-up and flew a consignment of shrimp in our only plane and this was the coup-de-grace that put us out of business. We couldn't fly anything but shrimp after that; they wouldn't even let us belly up to a hangar. We had to park our crate out far afield, and downwind. We stunk even worse than business. It felt fine now, remembering it, though. There were worse times. We were our own mechanics. If our plane developed engine trouble in Central America, we had to fly down there and repair it ourselves. We could hitch air-rides, but couldn't afford to pay mechanics.

My mind moved forward, following that line of thought, the way it will sometime. You start with a simple thought and it'll drag you through a lot of complicated thoughts. Our air-freight line continued losing money and we went out of business and nobody noticed. I hooked on with an air-freight service that was larger than our operation: this boy owned three Air Force surplus planes.

I felt the sharp twist of agony. I could still feel this guy's fist twisted in my shirt pulling me up so I was as tall as he was. He had to hold me there because I was too potted to stand alone. You're fired, Johnson, you're fired, you damned drunk. Anybody who'd let you fly their planes is a damned fool and I'm no damned fool. I wriggled, I could speak distinctly enough to make him understand me, even if I couldn't make him care. I yelled at him. I can fly better dead drunk, I told him, than you can dead sober. His voice was hard, and all the old friendship we'd had during the war and after it was gone. Maybe you can, he said, but not for my company.

Sitting in the air-conditioned Rudder Room now, I ordered another drink, quick, trying to blur the pain of that memory. I had liked that guy. We had logged a lot of hours together. I had wanted him to like me because we'd been together a lot of times, a lot of places we could never forget, even when we tried. Besides, this was the nineteenth or twentieth job I'd had since they agreed to let me resign my Air Force commission, but even that wasn't what was important. This guy was a nice joe, and he was a flier, and I wanted to be a nice joe, and work around a guy that was my kind of flier. And he didn't want me around because when I took a drink with him, I couldn't stop drinking, and I was a lush and nobody trusted a lush when his chance of staying in business rode every time one of his planes took off. Hell, I couldn't even blame him.

I glared around the quiet room, hearing the piped-in music, seeing the bottles stacked so the indirect lighting danced in them, everything swank and quietly elegant, and me sitting there in it tormented and sweated because I was remembering something there was no sense remembering and all because some slob with a gimmick wouldn't let me alone.

I turned on the stool and looked at him, the pale hair, the pale lashes, the thin face. If ever a guy turned it to clabber . . .

"Why don't you get lost?" I said. I was louder than the music, louder than the rumble of a revving ship out on the runways. Ollie glanced up, polishing glasses behind the bar. Everybody knew Buz Johnson. He could be trouble when he got a load on.

Coates turned his glass upside down, trapping the olive under it and rolling it around on the damp bar.

"I don't know," he said. "Just trying to be friendly."

"I got my own friends."

"Sure you have. But you got any friends that can help you latch on to a hundred grand?"

My face twisted. I could feel it rutting, feel it twist, getting ugly so the ugliness hurt. I stared at the glass in my

15

fist. Then I threw it down on the bar so it smashed and shards flew. I waited, but Ollie didn't say anything. He was watching a big Eastern DC-7 out on a runway.

I walked out.

Chapter Five

I got off the bus at the corner of Crawley and walked east toward my apartment, my nostrils still clogged with the fumes from the bus's diesel engine. For me, this was one of the worst effects of being stranded on the ground, the smell of fumes and the people crowding you. Sometimes the whole city crowded me and I got claustrophobia standing in the middle of a street.

I heard the kids yelling, and somebody said that's where God is, in a kid's yell, but that isn't where God is for me. I felt the sun against my shoulders, sweating out the beer, dehydrating me. I'd thought I could get all the way home without a drink, but I saw now I wasn't going to be able to make it.

I felt the tensions and the town closing in, riding my shoulders. Sunpark wasn't a bad town, as good as any, fine if you thought any town was good. It had a lot of sunshine, about three hundred thousand people, and squatted on a rim of the Gulf of Mexico. There were tourists, and industry, and shipping and an Air Force base with jets smearing up the sky like a kid with wet chalk.

I walked past the entrance of my apartment house. Cars rattled the narrow street and the noon-smell of cooking almost smothered me. I saw old men sitting in the sun waiting for lunch and men talking outside small shops. I stepped around some little girls playing jacks on the walk and went in the Old Sarge's Bar on the corner of Eighth.

I blinked against the beer-cool darkness and saw the only customer in there at this hour was a woman. She sat at the far end of the bar staring into a beer glass and listening to the juke box beside her. I didn't check her because I have one other weakness, too—just any doll won't do. But I didn't want to get involved in that line of thought, either.

I leaned against the bar between two stools because I owed the Old Sarge some money and I didn't want him to think I could pay off or that I meant to order without admitting I was already on the cuff. These matters are delicate.

"Hi, Major." The Old Sarge smiled. His face had the look of rare roast beef and wrinkled up around the eyes when he smiled.

He was polishing glasses, a big man with chunky hands and beefy shoulders, too bulky for the space behind the bar, too big for his whole establishment. The bar was a curved deal along the side of a wall. There were a couple of booths, a few tables, a television set strung from the ceiling, and the juke box glowing like a chameleon. Old Sarge had once displayed a life-size nude behind the bar, something he had found in Italy during the war and lugged through hell to get back here to his place. He said he had gone all through the war thinking how that Italian nude was going to dress up his place when he returned to Sunpark. He'd owned this same bar before they drafted him. But then it had been called The Friendly Bar. He had changed the name when he got home and hung up his nude. The bluenoses had made him take it down four or five years ago.

"Hello, Sarge," I said. "I'm not fixed to pay up, but I wondered how bad shape my credit is in?"

He shrugged. "Hell, Major. Four or five weeks. Nothing."

"You know, Sarge, you're first on my list. The minute—"

"Look. I know that. Am I hounding you?"

"It's not that. It's a thirsty day."

"Say, what's the matter with you, Major? If you can't come here for a few drinks, what the hell? I know you'll pay me. Good Lord, last time how long was it?"

"You're trying to embarrass me," I said, perching one cheek on a stool.

"Hell, Major, you know better than that. Look. My wife. You know my wife. God, you don't have to answer that. Everybody this end of town knows my wife—like they used to know the air-raid sirens during the war. Look. Not even my wife worries about your tab. She keeps the books. She raises hell about Reilly, about the Dago. She never has mentioned you one time. Not one time. I'll tell you what, we'll run your tab until my wife complains. How's that? That way it don't have to be between us and don't have to talk about it. Okay?"

"I think that sounds fine." I dampened my lips and he poured me a double bourbon and a beer chaser.

"Not many guys left around here who're like us, Major. Like you and me—guys I can talk to. Not any more. I swear, I don't know what happens to them. Some guys are dead, but some of the others—they act like what we went through never even happened. They don't even care about it any more."

"They never did care, Sarge."

"Why should they? They sat on their fat 4-F behinds, walked around on their flat feet and made more damned money than they could even spend. Why should they care?"

"I don't know."

"You know, Major. It's too bad you were commissioned. You could have had one hell of a good time if you'd been a non-com."

"No. I wouldn't have gotten to fly."

"Yeah. That's true. Of you. Maybe the officers in the Air Force weren't such stupid bastards as in the Army anyhow. In the Navy now I heard most of the officers had pretty good sense. Most of them just stayed out of the way and let the petty officers run things. And if you don't think the petty officers run the Navy, you just never been in it. Guy in here said their exec stayed in his sack, or at the coffee urn in officer's country and you couldn't find him without radar. The only decisions he would make would be if port side or starboard got first liberty. Anything more than that, he'd get clabbery diarrhea."

"Most of us were just guys trying to do what they told us. Most of us didn't know how."

"Except you. You knew how to handle those planes. Eh, Major?"

I moved the beer mug around on the cool bar. "I guess that was the only time I was ever worth a damn. I thought I was flying for some reason, doing some good. And I came back home to find out I was doing it because I was a jerk without influence enough to get out of it."

"You had a lot of company, Major."

"Yeah. That's what made it fine. The best guys in the world were the poor sons of bitches who didn't have influence enough to get out of being there. We really lived, Sarge."

He kept refilling my glasses. I got to thinking about the war in the Pacific, and later the retread action I'd had in Korea. At the time, it had been hell. But it didn't seem like hell now. I needed those wars. I accomplished something. Some men look back to the town where they were born, the first girl they loved. Me? I seemed to wake up, to come alive when I arrived at that flight school in Georgia. 1942. August. I had a purpose in life. I drank then. We all did. But it was different because we didn't need to drink. We had something else first. Something I didn't have any more.

Sometimes, it seemed to me, a man needed one more war. They took everything else away from him, the bastards who walked the ground. They hated you and tried to drag you down and show you what a nothing you were without your plane and your war. It got so you remembered the odds against you as a good thing, a chance to live high and go out fast. It sounds trite now, but it was true—so true that it became trite. Just the same, being shot from the air wasn't the worst way to die. Every man got it sometime—and the slow way with the smiling Jimmy Clarks riding you because if he didn't he would feel inferior and he couldn't stand that—could be a lot worse. During the war, you remembered, you lived high, drank hard, spent free. A man couldn't want any more than that.

I was telling them about the time I took off from a carrier in the Coral Sea. The woman had moved up the bar beside me and was listening as intently as the Sarge. It seemed fine that she would care enough to listen. Maybe she was rather chubby, but she was really very pretty.

I got off the stool and walked back and forth before it, telling them, remembering how it had been. I was seeing it. I sweated. I didn't know how I had gotten started talking about it. But I was glad. It seemed funny as hell now, and they were laughing, seeing how funny it was.

"I flew until I had twenty minutes' gas left and that was when I got back to rendezvous. Only there wasn't anything to rendezvous with. For God's sake, I stared down there and the stinking carrier was just going down for the third time in flames and oil fires. Poor bastards were swimming around in the oil, looking up at me as if I could help them and I was up there without any gas for Christ's sake."

"What did you do?" the woman said.

"Hell, I flew to Pearl Harbor and got help. What else?"

They laughed. The Sarge said, "Errol Flynn was there, wasn't he, Major? At Pearl, I mean?"

"Sure. Man, when I found out he was there, that was all I needed. We sent the task force home, mopped up alone."

"You said you didn't have any gas," the woman said.

"That was the sad part," the Sarge told her. "He didn't have any gas."

"I didn't have Errol Flynn, either."

"It must have been hell," the woman said.

"Hell?" I stared at her. "It was the most wonderful time of my life."

"But—you had to—to ditch the plane, didn't you?"

"What the hell? There were plenty other guys down in that water. I didn't get any wetter than they did."

I looked around. I didn't recognize the room. It was a frilly cubicle with white curtains and venetian blinds drawn tightly. It looked like the transient sort of place you might rent in somebody's shabby apartment hotel. At the same time there were signs it had been lived in for a long time. Feminine undergarments were tossed around and the overwhelming scent of toilet water and mascara washed over me.

I shook my head.

"What's the matter, honey?" the woman said.

I was sitting on the side of the bed. I wiped my hand across my face.

"How'd I get here?"

"You kidding? You came with me."

I didn't say anything.

"Don't you like me?" she said.

"Sure. You're fine."

I stared up at her. I had no memory of leaving the Old Sarge's Bar. I had no memory of her, either. I hadn't even wanted to pick her up. Yet here I was. She still had her dress on, but she was working at it. She lowered her voice telling me I could have anything I wanted. Only I didn't want anything. I looked at her, trying to want her as she pulled away the filmy print frock and began to spill out of it, white and full and scented. I kept telling myself how easy it was. Easy. When you got down to it, it was as easy as opening a door. You just had to reach over and lift the latch.

She smiled at me. She was pretty. She wasn't in her twenties any more but she hadn't been out of them very long. There was a soft look about her eyes, and a hurt in them. That shoved me way out. I wanted nothing to do with soft, hurt eyes.

"I'm sorry," I said.

"What's the matter, love?"

"Nothing."

"Do you think I'm pretty?"

"Whether I think so or not, you are pretty." I smiled, thinking you could follow her down into hell and never look around or feel the heat.

"Just tell me you think I'm pretty," she said. "You can have anything you want."

I wiped my hand across my mouth.

She stepped out of her dress as if she'd been doing it for fun all her life.

I shook my head. I stood up, walked toward the door. She touched my arm. Otherwise she didn't try to stop me. I smiled at her. I wished I had some present to leave with her. But that was the story of my life. I could hurt people, but I could never do anything the way I wanted.

"Just any doll," she said.

"What?"

"Just any doll," she repeated in that lifeless tone. "That's what you've been saying ever since we left the Sarge's. You didn't want just any doll."

I touched the doorknob. "I guess that's the way it is. It's not your fault."

She sighed. "In a way it is. I should have left you alone. But I kept telling myself I wasn't just any doll, that I was something special."

I looked at her. There wasn't anything else to say. I

21

opened the door and walked out. She closed it very softly behind me.

I woke up yelling.

As soon as I was awake, I rolled over, wiped the sweat off my face without opening my eyes. I cursed myself for yelling, but I didn't really care. I was used to the dream by now, used to the yelling that went with it. It was a recurring dream, in Technicolor, and I don't give a damn how unlikely the psychiatrists say this is. In fact, it had been a psychiatrist who suggested I resign my commission in the Air Force. And all because of that same old dream. It had started its playing dates in my sleep like a first-run movie during the war, and kept playing the same old circuit, scratchy prints and jumbled sequences but with all the same old impact of horror. Only during the war I'd had a different name for it.

In those days I had called it a nightmare.

This was the change, my attitude toward it. Dreaming that I was plummeting downward in flames, unable to move or aid myself, certainly ought to qualify as a nightmare. But I did not feel this way any more. When it happened now, it was a familiar show. It was like returning to a place full of memories that no longer had any agony in them. Now the dream, and the sweats, and the sure knowledge that I'd screamed myself awake was no longer torture. It got so that a man's waking world was a torment so he had to run back, away from it, and the events that had once seemed evil weren't so bad any more. One more war? I figured that was what my dream meant. That's what it had to mean; otherwise my being shot down in flames didn't mean anything. The wars were over for me and this wasn't the way I was slated to die.

I heard some faint movement in the room or in the corridor but I didn't open my eyes. Probably somebody had heard me yell and was running around out there, troubled but unable to find any place to stick his nose.

"You have dreams like that very often?"

I lunged upward in bed, my eyes wide and staring. It was late afternoon. The sunlight streamed in a dusty shaft through the west window.

Sid Coates was sitting in a straight chair that he had pulled up beside my bed. He looked like some apparition from a horror movie, the dangling lock of bleached hair, the pale brows and that silly grin that pulled his face out of shape.

"What are you doing here?"

"Having a drink," Coates said. He held up one of the pint bottles I kept hidden around the place for mad liquor.

"How'd you find that?"

"It wasn't easy."

I could feel the anger building. "How'd you get in here?"

He shrugged. "You're wasting time with non-essentials. Getting in anywhere is easy if you've got charm enough."

"You fail to charm me."

"That's just because you don't know me."

"That's the way I want to leave it, too."

"I once charmed my way out of a four-year reformatory rap. Would you like to hear about that?"

"No."

"Some other time then. It's a fact, though, nobody can resist Sid Coates when he turns on the charm."

"I'll fight myself."

He shook that lock of hair off his forehead and took another pull at the bottle.

"A lot of people do," he said, grinning at me. "But it doesn't help. You see, in college I was a psychology major. So I find out what will charm each person and I use that approach. It is very simple, really, because though people all think they're so individual, they're all pretty much alike."

"Get out of here."

He seemed not even to hear me. "Now, you take my mother. She's a dear woman. As stupid as a cat. You see, it isn't truly her fault—the stupidity, I mean. Her folks had money. They protected her from every fact of life. Hell, I doubt if she learned to wave bye-bye until she was fifteen. But to this day she believes all the axioms from the book of social usage. People are so and so. They must do so and so. There are people who come to the front door, the side door and the back door. Nothing must ever happen to upset this plan. I've been a deep and bitter disappointment to her.

23

She tries to hate me. But just for the hell of it, I won't let her. I charm the old girl right out of her skin. And I do it just for the hell of it. I could take the money from her if I wanted to. She couldn't punch her way out of a bag."

"Shut up, will you?"

"Here. Have a drink." He extended my pint bottle. There were not more than two drinks left in it.

"You've really been nursing this thing."

"Just amusing myself while I waited. Now if you're wide awake, we can get down to business. We have a lot to talk about."

Chapter Six

"You got holes in your head coming here like this, Coates," I told him, "and I'd have to have matching holes to listen to you."

He grinned and it was a wild, other-side-of-the-moon grimace, that grin. I kept expecting him to tell me to take him to my leader. He would push his fingers through that pale lock of hair and then it would topple right back where it had been; only it was becoming sweated and lank now every time it brushed against his wet forehead.

"I figure you have," Coates said. "Man, I'm a lot of things. But one of them ain't stupid."

"Then get out of here."

"Suppose I came in here to sell you a set of encyclopedias or a brush," Coates said. "You'd listen, wouldn't you?"

I took the bottle, drank deeply. Once the liquor began to burn through me, I felt better. This clown was a clown, but by now, I'd decided he was harmless. A lot of times a drink will do this for you. One more drink is often just what you need.

"You got three more minutes," I said. I swung out of bed, went to the bathroom, came back. Coates had been talking when I walked out of the room, and he was still talking when I returned.

"—so my old man hasn't spoken to me since they kicked me out of the university. The only time I get to see my mother is when the old boy is out of the house, and it's safer when he's out of town. This makes it inconvenient, because I can't always arrange my finances to suit his trips away from home. So, I told you all this so you'd know who I am, and where I came from, and all the things you'd have to know about any man with whom you went into partnership."

I stared at myself in a mirror and shuddered. I stuck out my tongue. It was white.

He watched me push military brushes through my hair.

"For a long time, Buz, I've had this plan. But I kept quiet about it. I never breathed a word of it, even when I was drunkest. Because I knew sometime I'd meet the guy who could help me pull it off, and I'd be set. Then I heard about you. Buz Johnson. Thirty-three. Ex-major in the Air Force. Ex-passenger service pilot. Every job I ever heard you had, you had just lost or just quit. Well, none of that sold me on you. It didn't prejudice me in any way, you understand. But it didn't prove either that you had the qualities I was seeking in a partner."

My shirt was a mess. I couldn't wear it any more. It looked as though I'd been sleeping in it. I unbuttoned it.

"No. I had to do a lot more investigating. Then I found out what I needed to know. Ex-Major Johnson liked to live high, liked to pay for the drinks, liked to have fast women and new cars or vice versa. In short, ex-Major Johnson liked all the things he had been almost able to afford on his major's pay. Only—since the fighting stopped, Johnson hadn't had his major's pay any more. So that's what I was looking for. That's when I figured you and I were alike—"

"Alike? You and me? God forbid."

He grinned. "Oh, I know. That's what everybody says at first thought. It's nauseating, I admit. But there it is—we're two of a kind."

I wadded up the shirt and threw it on a chair.

"You see, Buz, we both have to have money. Oh, I don't mean a few dollars. Beer money. Money in the wallet. Money for medical expenses. That crap. We need enough dough so we don't have to think about it any more."

"This makes us alike? You name me somebody who doesn't need money this way."

"Plenty of people, Buz. Hell, there are millions of people

who never expect to have anything. They expect to live in a rut with just enough to squeeze by on, or not quite enough. They like it that way. They'd be frightened if anything else happened."

I went back to the bathroom. I loosened my pants to step out of them so I could get a shower, but Coates followed and leaned on the doorjamb behind me. I forgot the shower, zipped my pants, buckled the belt, washed my face and under my arms. I still felt sweaty.

"But I want money for cars, and dames, and clothes. I tell you, man, I get a fever when I look at the new styles that come out all the time. I feel naked walking the street in last year's suit. You can dig that, can't you, Major? I want money. I want a big wad of it. I want it now. I haven't the time or the inclination to work and save and accumulate a damned fortune by saving and investing and sweating. Christ, I'm young, and now is when I need money. When I get old I'll sit around and live on a Social Security check."

"What Social Security check?"

"Oh, they'll have them for moral outcasts by the time I'm 65," he said. "But that's not what's on my mind. It's now. This present. My old man refuses me cigarette money. My old lady is a little better, but still a tightwad. Even if she weren't, it wouldn't help. She can let me have only so little or the old man raises hell with her. I wouldn't care about that, except that when he clamps down on her, she puts the screws to me—with lectures."

I pushed past him and went back to the bedroom. I stood at the window, praying for fresh air, and having that prayer denied, too.

He followed me. "And then I heard about you. You want all the things you had when you roared around hell-on-wheels on a major's flight pay. You want to buy for the boys, gift the girls, be a hell of a fellow—and you make sixty stinking bucks a week. I felt sorry for you when I heard about it."

"You don't have to feel sorry for me, boy."

"I don't. Not any more. Because now we're together. You and me. Man, when I saw you the first time, it was as though we'd grown up together, as if I'd known you all my life. There was something about you that was more familiar to me than anybody in my own family."

"What do I do, thank you or take a poke at you?"

He smiled. "That's better, Major. Coming around now? Beginning to see that maybe we are alike—"

"Look. I can't go on listening to you if you're going to keep up that jazz about us being alike."

He laughed. "All right. We're in the same boat. We were meant to be partners."

"You're nuts."

"What's that got to do with it? Buz, my friend, I may be a little eccentric, but then most men of genius are."

"You're also a genius?"

"What else? Wait until you hear the first installment of my plan for instant wealth for two. I'll even allow you to suspend judgment on my genius until you hear it."

I turned, leaned against the window sill and stared at him. He stood tall and lean, stoop-shouldered, his bleached hair lank and damp.

His voice shook slightly with the excitement in it. "Buz, you don't know. The number of times I've been over this thing in my mind. The way I've known it would work. But the way I've needed somebody else I could trust to help me put it over. This is it, Buz. And what makes it genius, and perfect, is that it's so damned simple. You and I and a plane—"

"Where do we get a plane?"

"We steal one if we have to. What the hell? Wait until you see what we can get with just one plane. I was in this hick town and looked the bank over. It's like a sardine can. I know how many blocks to the highway, how many roads lead out of town, where they go, what condition they're in. I know where a plane could be brought down attracting almost no attention, and yet would be accessible to the bank. I know how many cops there are in that town. Two. Not counting the state highway patrolman who rides through there maybe every other day. I even heard they've never even had a filling-station robbery in that hickville in over forty years. Robbery is the last thing these hicks ever think about.

"And this is what makes it so perfect, Buz. If they did think about robbery they'd think about it in simple terms of something they could comprehend, a man on foot, a man

27

in a car, a man on horseback, maybe. But in an airplane?" He laughed and slapped his leg. "They wouldn't believe it, even while they watched it. It would be like seeing a man from Mars to them. And that's what would make it so perfect. We could hide the plane, get in the bank, load ourselves with that gorgeous green stuff and take off. While they ran around looking for car tracks, we'd be off in the wild blue yonder. Now tell me, Major, does that sound like genius?"

"It might work."

"Might work? What's to fail? Are you nuts? It's perfect and it's simple. It's got to work."

"That's where you're wrong. No matter how stupid they are, they'll remember you—"

"We wear dark glasses on the street. Dark glasses in the bank. And that's where the plane comes in. We fix an alibi—ninety miles away. We might have a little trouble with a few minutes of it, but not enough to place us definitely in that hick town. It would sound impossible."

"Sure. Unless somebody said, Buz Johnson was in on it. Buz Johnson could fly a plane over there and back in that questioned time. And that's what they would say."

"You're nuts. Why would they even suspect you?"

"I don't know. But if they did, there would be their answer."

"There's no reason for them to suspect you. A town a hundred miles away. A robbery. A getaway in a car. They find the abandoned car, and that's the end of the trail."

"What about the weather?"

"What?"

"What about the weather?"

"What about it? What's the weather got to do with it?"

"Everything. If it were bad enough, we'd be grounded. If it were too good, there would be a sky full of planes."

"So what? We'd be just another plane."

"Not if the plane were stolen. What is the owner of the plane going to do while we use it? He'll report it, and they'll be looking for it."

"So. Have you got a better idea?"

"Yeah. Drop the whole thing. Any time a man comes to me with a plan that has to do with flying and he's too stupid even to figure in the weather—that's all I need to hear."

"How in hell would I know what the weather would be?"

"You'd find out. That's how in hell you'd know. You wouldn't make your first move until you did know."

"All right. I'll buy that."

I stared at him. Did he think I was nuts enough to go for a chowderhead plan like this? Obviously he did. He was sweating, even trembling slightly with his inner excitement.

"The hell with you," I said. "I was just showing you the holes in your plan. I was just trying to keep you from getting your tail full of lead. I wouldn't touch it."

"All right. Maybe it is a little rough around the edges—"

"A little rough? My God. You got to consider everything—but the weather most of all when you're flying. You got to know how far to the nearest airport, the nearest place you could stash the plane . . . Go on, get out of here."

Coates was laughing. "You've thought of a caper like this before."

I didn't answer for a moment. In that time I seemed to see Jimmy Clark's snarling smile, the Glad Hand Finance Company offices, the Old Sarge's bar, this room.

"Yeah," I said after what seemed a long time to me. "I've thought about it."

"So. All right. So here's our chance to make a killing."

I shook my head. "A guy thinks about a lot of things when he gets broke or drunk—or both. That don't mean I'd touch your idea. I got just one thing to say to you, Coates."

"Yeah? What's that, ole buddy?"

"Get out of here."

Chapter Seven

The next morning at seven o'clock the telephone rang. I tried to outwait it and couldn't. Finally I rolled over in bed and lifted the receiver. It was Coates. I immediately recognized that silly laugh. "You've had most of the night to think it over, ole buddy—"

I slapped down the receiver. I lay there a long time. It had the feel of another hot day, dry, still air and an early morning glare on everything beyond my windows. At last I got up, showered and dressed. I admitted I had not slept all night, but it had nothing to do with Coates and his fool plan. It was just that everything was adding up, crowding in with time running out, like a drink tab you're unable to pay three minutes before closing in some swank bar.

I went down to the cafe on the corner for breakfast, but when I got there I wasn't hungry. I had a cup of coffee and then went out, carrying my leather jacket across my shoulder, to wait for a bus. Suddenly I couldn't do it. I couldn't ride a crowded bus this morning. It was the one thing I couldn't take. At least a dozen people were at the bus stop waiting with me and only God knew how many would be jammed and sweating in the bus when it finally arrived.

I rammed my hand in my pocket, counted my change. I had just enough for a cab to the airport and a dime tip. It was a hell of a lousy tip, all right. I remembered times in Paris when we had thrown francs at the taxi men. Francs had no more value than soap coupons to us. They weren't real, and it wouldn't have mattered if they were real.

I got out of the cab at the terminal building at Sunpark International. I walked through it, hearing the people chattering and hurrying, all of them going somewhere, and buying insurance before they took off. There was a racket I wished I was in; it rated just slightly under owning Texas oil wells.

I went out the baggage exit and walked toward Hangar 2 where Jimmy Clark's face beamed down in phony benevolence on everything.

I stopped walking. It had nothing to do with the sign. It was Judy. I felt the muscles in my stomach go taut. She was standing over there, trim and lovely in her stewardess uniform, talking with Jimmy Clark. She had her back to me, and for a moment I marveled at the soft way her hair grew from under her cap and along the nape of her neck. I knew it was Judy; I would know her around a corner. I didn't need to see her. I could sense her nearness. It had been this way for a long time, a long, hopeless time.

Right now, though, I didn't want her to see me. There was no reason for it, but her being there talking to Jimmy

Clark angered me. Besides, talking to her never got us anywhere any more.

I turned on my heel and walked back toward the lobby. I was almost there when I heard her speak my name.

"Buz."

"Oh. Hello."

"You were running away from me," she said. She had a voice that hurt you somehow. It was throaty and had just the touch of violins. I had it bad? Sure. I'd had it bad for a long time.

"You were talking to Jimmy."

"I was waiting for you."

"I hope so. I hate to think you hang around Jimmy Clark from choice."

She bit at her lip. "Please don't, Buz. He is my stepfather whether you like it or not."

"I'm glad I don't have to like it."

"He's always been very nice to me."

"I'll bet."

"Oh, Buz. Can't you get rid of the hate talk? How can you think such things?"

I shrugged. "Well, here we go again. So long, Judy."

"Buz, wait."

I stopped. The glare of the sun was painful against my eyes. I felt them sting.

"I wanted to talk to you, Buz," she said.

"Well, there's always my bed. Why don't you come up?"

"Oh, no, Buz. I told you. Not any more. Not ever any more."

My jaw tightened. "Yes. You've told me. In fact, it seems to me you get some kind of perverse pleasure from telling me."

"Oh, Buz, that isn't true. I loved you once. I think I'm still in love with you now."

"Sure."

"But it's impossible, Buz. I—I'm sorry but I can't throw my life away."

I exhaled. "Now you begin to sound like Jimmy Clark."

"I'm sorry. It's just that I can't stand it when we hurt each other. That's why I know we shouldn't see each other. We only hurt each other every time."

"All right. Like you said. I was running away from you."

Her deep eyes showed tears. We both pretended to ignore them.

"Are you all right, Buz? You know what I mean."

"Good Lord, the bars don't even open until nine."

"I know. But you don't always wait."

I stared at the backs of my hands. "How could you ever have loved me and think what you do about me?"

"Well, I did love you. Not for the mistakes you kept making, but for what you were really, Buz—what you could be." She stared at me—then, with effort, made her voice relax. "But I did want you to be sober this morning."

"Why? Isn't this a day like all other days?"

She touched my arm. "Inside the lobby, Buz. A friend of yours. An old friend. I didn't want you to see him though— if you'd been drinking."

"You'd make a fine mother hen. You know that, don't you?"

"Oh, yes. I know what I am, all right." She gave me a turn and gently shoved me toward the lobby doors. She turned then and walked back toward Hangar 2 where I saw Jimmy Clark watching us, unsmiling.

I went through the glass doors, glanced toward the lunch counter which was crowded, the waiting area which was crowded, children crying and women looking bedraggled even in the air conditioning. I saw no one I knew and wondered what to do until Judy left Hangar 2 and I could go to my purgatory in peace. The Rudder Room topside wasn't opened yet, wouldn't be for another hour. If Ollie were up there, I might rattle a door until he let me in.

But I despised the idea of sitting surrounded by that much alcohol as broke as I was. It was Thursday and Clark would delay paying me until as late as possible Friday afternoon, and most of that pay was gone already. Ollie could run a tab for me, but if he were caught, he could lose his job, too. He would take a chance for me, but I couldn't ask him to.

"Hey, Buz! Chicken. Chicken Johnson. Is that you, boy?"

I heeled around, hearing a voice that was like something out of one of my purple nightmares.

Greenie was running toward me. His swarthy face was

pulled into a twisted grin. In that moment all I could see was that the poor bastard was getting old. He was getting bald, and fat.

"Greenie. Good Lord. Greenie."

I caught him in my arms and hoisted him from the floor. This caused all the hurried people in the place to pause and stare and laugh because, although Greenie was only a couple inches taller than I, he weighed a good two hundred pounds. "Man, are you getting fat."

He laughed, pounding me on the back. "Son, I'm eating more chicken than a preacher." He glanced over his shoulder and I noticed the two Latin types he'd been standing with. They were runty men, and oily, but their clothes had the expensive look about them that can't be faked. "Is there some place we can talk, Buz? I'm between planes. We're riding ASA south this morning. I sure would like to talk to you a few minutes."

"Sure," I said. "We can go up to the Rudder Room. It isn't open yet. I'll get it opened."

He grinned and slapped my shoulder. But something odd flickered in his face. "Never was a bar you couldn't open up, eh, Buz?"

"I reckon we've done some drinking together."

"A long time ago, Buz."

He walked back to where his Latin boys stood watching him as if they were frightened and lost without him. I saw them gesticulating and glancing at their watches. He argued them down and then came back, carrying his coat across his arm. His suit was well-tailored, too. Greenie looked as if he were in the money. Only, for the first time I noticed that he needed a shave and probably hadn't slept all night on whatever flight had brought him in.

We sat in a booth in the Rudder Room. Ollie brought us a bottle of whisky and went away. Greenie said, "Just some mineral water for me, huh?" Ollie nodded and brought it.

"What happened to you and whisky, Greenie?" I said, gesturing a salute before I drank off the first one.

He frowned, watching me. "Just—don't need it any more, Buz." He glanced around, looked at his watch. He said he didn't have time for anything but a quick recap of the past ten years since we'd seen each other. We tried, but we couldn't stay away from the hellish times we'd had together in the Air Force.

Thinking about it, I poured a double.

"How are things with you, Buz?"

I almost lied, involuntarily. The whisky had struck my empty stomach and reverberated to the top of my skull. After all, Greenie was just passing through. He was riding high; this was obvious. Why bore him with my woes? Besides, I never had liked admitting I couldn't even buy an old friend a drink.

"I'm doing all right." I reached for the bottle.

He touched my arm. "You hittin' this stuff pretty heavy?"

"For God's sake, what's heavy?"

He laughed after a moment. "Yeah. That's right." He glanced at his watch again. "It was just that I'd heard you were off the stuff, Buz."

"Hell, where'd you ever pick up a canard like that? I told you. I'm doing all right."

"What's all right?"

"I get by."

"Get by? Buz, that's not good enough for you. Look, you saw the clowns downstairs I'm with. They're from a fancy SA republic. They want to improve their airline down there. Nothing fancy. Just TWA with chrome. I've been running it for them. And it's coming along. You wouldn't believe it. Buz, we're up here placing orders for new DC-7's, and we'll have the first jet service down there. It's a big operation and it's rich. And there's a place for you, Buz. Jesus. That goes without saying. Anywhere I am, there's a place for you."

I pushed the bottle away. "You haven't much time, Greenie. I'll level. I've been fired by all the big ones. I drink pretty hard—no matter what you heard. It's nothing I want to do. But here it is."

"Hell, Buz. You can lay it down, like you picked it up. I know. You think I haven't heard about you in these past years? Sure, you drank. You've lost jobs. But you never worked an operation like this—so big it takes the place of drinking. Man, at first I had a hell of a time staying sober. But then I got busy. I was working hard at something I

34

loved, I was accomplishing something, making something big out of nothing. Hell, now I can drink once in a while, or never."

"You got it made," I said.

The p.a. system announced the ASA flight. He stood up. He found a card in his coat pocket, scribbled his address on it. "Buz, you listen. Come to work for me. High pay. Good hours. Wonderful planes. And you're working for me—I'll give you a chance to dry out if you need it. You'll be on the payroll and nobody can get to you boy, except through me. Don't make up your mind right now. You keep this card. Wire me. I'll send you expense money—an advance. I'll get you down there—and boy, it'll be like Army days—only with real money, no bullets, and an air service that just grows and grows. You think it over, you hear?"

He dropped the card on the table, tossed a fifty dollar bill on top of it to cover the tab, knowing damned well I'd keep the change, wanting me to. He slapped me on the shoulder again. His eyes glistened and he grinned. "We gave 'em hell, didn't we, Buz?"

He grabbed up his coat and then he was gone.

Chapter Eight

I sat there for a long time after Greenie left, sat with that fifty dollar bill crushed in my fist. Finally I paid Ollie, tipping him handsomely and walked slowly down the steps. Greenie was gone and I had a sense of loss and emptiness. It was lost, all of it, all we'd had, all we'd done. Even the men we had been, they were gone too. And what was left? A good-hearted guy named Greenie offering charity to a guy he once had loved.

For a moment I couldn't help seeing the way it would be to have money again, a real ship to fly, something to accomplish. My hands shook. I rammed them in my pockets, touching the money Greenie had left me.

"Buz."

I shivered and had an impulse to run. I didn't want to see her. Why in hell couldn't she let me alone?

I turned. Her smile was like something someone had painted on crookedly.

"How'd it go, Buz?"

"Greenie? Oh, we had a drink together. Hacked up old memories."

"He didn't say anything else?" Her voice was flat. I looked at her, the soft, violet-blue eyes, the flesh with the glowing tint to it, and the stewardess uniform that could do nothing to her body except accentuate it. For a moment I didn't say anything. She was as tall as I and her eyes held mine levelly.

I pretended to glance around the lobby. "Where is Jimmy Clark?" I said. "Since when does he allow you talk to me out of his sight?"

"Are things so bad with you and Jimmy, Buz?"

"How else would they be? He hates my guts. He's also afraid I might touch you, He's got the damned fool idea you're nuts about me."

"Where'd he ever get an idea like that?"

"Not from me."

"No. Not from you."

She touched my arm, led me across the gleaming terrazzo floor to a leather couch that had just been vacated. Through the floor-to-ceiling windows I could see the commercial planes out on the runways. Without intending to, I looked for the ASA flight. It was far down a runway, charging up for the take-off into the wind. I shivered.

"I came in this morning," Judy said. Her hand was still on my arm. I pretended to scratch my cheek so I could covertly bump her hand away. I saw her bite her lip, then smile quickly. "As I told you, I was on the plane with a friend of yours."

I felt the chill deepen.

"Greenie," she said. "How many times I've heard you talk about him. Greenie. The times you two used to have together. I saw his name on the manifest. I asked if he had ever been a pilot. Buz, when I mentioned you, I couldn't get away from him. He wouldn't stop talking. He really thinks you're wonderful."

I stared at my clenched fists. "I suppose you told him all about me? How I've quit drinking and all that?"

"What do you mean, Buz?"

"You know damned well what I mean. That I haven't two bucks, that I can't even ask the girl I love to marry me, that the job I have depends on how much crap I can take. Did you ask Greenie to hire me?"

"Oh, no, Buz. I didn't. He said he was looking for you. He'd been looking for you for years. He didn't think he'd have time to see you. He asked me to tell you to get in touch with him at once."

"Well, I saw him."

"I know. Oh, Buz. I'm so glad for you."

"Are you?"

"You are going to take the job, aren't you, Buz?"

"What job?"

"Oh, Buz. He wanted to give you a job. With his airline. A really good job, with flight pay—"

"You really covered all the details, didn't you?"

She bit her lip again. "Shouldn't I have, Buz? Should I pretend I wasn't interested? Of course I'm interested."

"So interested you told him I'd quit drinking, begged him to hire me?"

"Buz, no."

I cursed. "I don't want his damned charity."

"Buz, it's not charity. It's a firm offer. He needs good fliers."

"Sure. But not drunks. You talked him into this little charity, didn't you?"

"Buz, you're not a drunk. You don't need to be. You could be anything—if you had the chance."

"Is that the line you gave Greenie?"

"Oh, Buz. You don't want to go on like this. Where is your pride?"

Pride? There was a lovely word. Sometimes I asked myself about my pride. I was made of it, ninety-nine percent, I was a proud man. But I'd lost all right to pride. I was beaten and dejected and I tried consciously to ignore my pride until someone pushed me too hard, too far. Then I raged back and no matter what common sense might dictate, there I was, the proud man, getting his nose broken, his teeth smashed, but proud.

She twisted her hands. "Why must you be cruel, Buz? To

yourself and to me. Greenie did want to hire you. He was looking for you. But whether he was or not, it's too good a job to pass up."

"I don't need you to go around begging jobs for me from my old friends," I said. "If there's anything you'd do well to remember, Judy, that's it."

"I'm sorry, Buz. I was just trying to help."

"I don't want your help."

"What do you want, Buz?" Her eyes shimmered with tears.

I stared at her, knowing I loved her more than anyone else had ever loved. Thousands of unfortunates are born with defects; mine was that I could love only this one girl. Hell, didn't I stay with Jimmy Clark for one more reason—she was his stepdaughter, and every third day she came into Sunpark and there was a chance to see her. You see, what you do is, you bang your head against a wall and keep banging it. But I knew how hopeless it was, too. Jimmy Clark had even told me frequently about the young pilot Judy dated in New York, all for my own good, of course.

My trouble was that you can live only so long with hopelessness and frustration. Then you start to hit back. The hell of it is you hit at the one you love. You want to flog that love to death, get it away from you, so you don't have to look at it any more. Well, I'd pretty much done that with Judy by now. Sometimes when she was in Sunpark between flights, we didn't see each other at all. She would call me and we would talk maybe thirty minutes, but about the time it seemed as if we had to see each other, the hurt would creep in, and one of us would hang up. It had been almost two weeks this time since I'd last seen Judy, except in the distance, except talking with Jimmy Clark, going out with her flight—to New York and her stalwart young pilot whom she never mentioned, but about whom I got all the late news from Jimmy Clark.

I pulled my gaze away from her and glared around the lobby. Sid Coates was standing near the entrance of the coffee shop. When he saw me recognize him, he grinned and walked toward us.

Angrily, I shook my head at him motioning him away. He was all I didn't need at that moment.

Judy turned, glancing toward Coates. She frowned. "Who is that man, Buz?"

"How do I know?"

"He knows you."

"So what? Everybody knows me. Buz Johnson. Big war ace. Ask Jimmy Clark."

"Please, Buz." She was watching Coates, still frowning. She sighed. "Buz, take that job."

"Why? You want me out of town?"

"I want you at work, Buz. Doing something you love. Gaining back your dignity and your self-respect."

"Sure. You'd like me to go down there and live on Greenie's charity, wouldn't you? Well. To hell with it. If I could go down there on equal terms with him, the way we were . . . Forget it, Judy, and from now on, quit begging jobs and charity for me."

"Buz, I didn't. I didn't."

I got up and walked away, leaving her sitting there.

Chapter Nine

Coates and I flew over this little back-country town the following Tuesday afternoon. For a change he kept his mouth shut most of the flight and I was glad. We couldn't spend too much time circling the town and though he swore he had cased it thoroughly, I wanted to get as clear a picture as possible in one quick run.

Fort Dale . . .

I observed carefully as we cruised over it. It was scarcely more than a village, like something somebody had hastily thrown together beside one of the cross-state highways, a place where a man could stop for a tank of gas, or a quick meal if he were desperately hungry. The main drag crossed the highway and the intersection showed four filling stations and a pigeon-pocked traffic signal that blinked day and night at nothing. To the east of the highway, this red-brick street ran past a few old houses and ended at a river where the bridge had collapsed and never been repaired. Beyond the river, cattle grazed in endless, flat, tan fields and birds grew fat in their wake.

This end of the street didn't interest me too much, but it was nice to know in advance that the street came to a dead end at the river. It was west of the highway, west of the four-block business section, west of the bank. . . . My heart pounded crazily when Coates nudged me and pointed out a narrow, red-brick building on a northwest corner. You'd never believe a carton like that would contain anything like two or three hundred grand. This back-country was deceptive. The people who lived out here made a lot of money from cattle and lumber and farming and orange groves, and they were a hundred miles from the nearest city where they might really spend it in considerable amounts. Fort Dale offered one movie theatre that operated three times a week, a couple of beer halls, a drugstore, and probably not even one really professional whore in the whole town.

I took it all in. I could not afford to be vague about anything down there. I made a pass over the place, took a long turn and did it again. I saw motel signs glittering in the metallic white sunlight, cars lining the hot streets, but mostly I saw the bank there, waiting for me. I lifted the Cessna and leveled out, cruising at less than a hundred.

"How does it look?" Coates said.

"It looks all right."

"No. I mean does it please you? The field I picked out to stash the plane is about half a mile west of the bank. There's a small farmhouse across the side road from the field but trees shield it so they couldn't see the field unless they happened to be out looking."

"All right."

"Does it please you?"

"I said okay."

"It looks all right to me. It's a long way from the nearest city. They'd be as likely to believe a man from Mars had landed if we came in by air. It looks fine to me. Of course if you don't buy it, we can case a few more towns—but I went over this one. I know the way in, the way out. How long it takes to get from the field to town—"

"And back?"

"We should be riding back in that stolen car."

"And the cops?"

40

"Except for the state patrol, there's a sheriff and a constable. We have to figure how to take them out of the game, and then as far as I'm concerned we're ready to pick up the marbles."

I didn't say anything.

"What's eating you now?" Coates wanted to know.

"Nothing."

"You like the place or not?"

I nodded. "It looks all right to me—from up here."

"And it looks even better when you're down there. I know, Buz. I've been over it. All of it. I drew out the plan from the field to town. It looks better down there. You want to drive over and look over it?"

"No. You've been over here already. I don't think we ought to fool around over here too much. Hicks in Hickville got an awful way of noticing every new man that walks into town."

"That's the way I feel. But I want you to buy the deal."

I exhaled, turning south by west. "When we've been over it a few times, maybe I'll buy it. The main thing I like about it right now is that there is no airport within fifty miles. When we take off, nobody's going to take off after us. No airport. No pursuit. That's what I like."

He laughed. "A hundred thousand waiting for us to pick it up. That's what I like."

I didn't say anything. We cruised back toward Sunpark and we were both thoughtful. Finally Coates laughed. "Man, I don't read you. First, you wouldn't touch this deal. Then you take over like it was born in you. And suddenly now you got nothing to say."

"I'm trying to think."

"What's there to think about?"

"There's plenty to think about, all right." I stared below at a small town about thirty miles inland from Sunpark. "That's Berry Town down there. Right?"

"Hell. How do I know?"

"You sure as hell better know. You better know everything there is to know about this country." I circled the town and flew over the airport, and then about six miles from this small town airfield with its half-dozen sport planes and forlorn windsock, I found what I was looking for.

I pointed it out to Coates. "Down there. An abandoned air strip. I thought I remembered landing in a spot like this once."

"Looks full of potholes. Would you try to land on it?"

"Nothing is easy, friend. I've landed in bigger potholes."

"Sure." Coates laughed. "That was why I wanted in this thing with you."

"Yeah," I said. "Now if we could figure why I wanted to have anything to do with you, we'd have it made."

"Because I'm the guy that will be there when you pull it off, that's why. I'm what you needed to get you started on a deal like this." He shook his head. "Only thing that beats me, Buz, is what made you change your mind."

I turned back toward Sunpark again and for a moment I didn't answer. Maybe because I didn't have the answer myself. The surest answer was that I could use a share of a hundred grand. But this wasn't the answer, didn't approach the answer. Why had I walked away from Judy with my mind made up to join Sid Coates in this robbery? Maybe it was because being around Judy now left me angered and frustrated, hating myself as much as anybody else, and needing violence. She was all I wanted, she was all I was never going to have. But a caper like this. No, I couldn't blame Judy because I was in it.

It had whirled and wheeled around in my brain for those two days, but it became a cold, hard knot, like an obstruction in my thinking processes while I was talking to Greenie. I made up my mind while I talked to him that I couldn't go down to South America, because I was a drunk digging his grave here in Sunpark. I wouldn't last. I needed something that would prove I still had strength and ability. Then, if I ever did go to work for Greenie in South America, I'd have a stake. I wouldn't be accepting his charity. If there had to be a reason for knocking over that bank in Fort Dale with Coates, that would have to be it.

Only I knew this wasn't all of it, either.

I envied Greenie. He'd had the look and feel of success about him; it was in the clothes he wore, the scent of expensive cigars and good after-shave lotion, the masculine deodorant that protected you without ostracizing you. He had everything I wanted—even to the haggard sleepless look in his eyes. He wasn't getting enough rest because he was working too hard at the one career he loved to take sack time. I wanted that. I hurt in my guts wanting to be slaving at something I loved. Hell, what I wanted was simple enough: I wanted a job that kept me busy around the clock, let me accomplish something. You could take everything else and you could ram it.

But the one thing Greenie had, I wanted most of all. The contempt he had for whisky. Christ, I trembled when I thought of being like that, not needing the stuff, not nursing the bottle, refusing a drink not because you were stuffy, but because you were high enough without it.

This was in my mind all the time. I had to let Greenie know that I didn't need Old Taylor for a crutch, because nothing can sour a man on you quicker than pity.

I glanced at the cars racing on the highway below me, a bunch of bastards down there, hurrying to nothing. Those sons of bitches who didn't care, and if they cared, they wanted to drag you down to their level just to show you how little they cared. I hated those ground-locked bastards and I wanted to show them I could make monkeys out of them. Monkeys on strings. Monkeys on leashes. Monkeys on ends of dirty sticks. And I wanted to prove something to myself. I didn't know exactly what it was, but when it was proved, I'd know it. I'd walk nine feet tall.

I glanced at Coates. I wasn't about to say any of this to him. Even if I could have said it, if I could string the words together so he would understand even part of what I meant, he wouldn't want to hear it. He wouldn't care.

I laughed. "I like the color of your eyes, baby," I said. "That's why."

"Sure you do," Coates said in a complacent voice. "How could you help it?"

I had checked into Sid Coates and what he really was as well as I could.

It was pretty easy to do in Sunpark. He had been born here, and drank in any alcohol dispensary, played pool anywhere there was a billiard table, picked up any girl who glanced back at him on the street.

I spent the next few days after talking with Greenie trying

to find out what made Coates tick. I can't say I found this out. What I found out was why he failed to tick at all.

He was an only child. His father was a circuit judge and his mother a clubwoman. As a child, Sid had a large store of energy and demanded a lot of attention. The world was a gay little place and he was the center of it..

By the time he was seven he began his career in military school. His mother was too delicate to cope with him—she got so that she was actually terrified of hearing what he had done next—and his father was too busy. They found the first of many military schools, and off he went. He was home only for a few days in the summer before they shipped him off alone to a summer military camp.

No matter what he asked his parents—those polite strangers whom he saw infrequently as he grew up—they answered him with a five dollar bill.

His first trouble was quite serious. He stole a car at thirteen and then charmed his way out of a term in reformatory. When he flunked out of his eighth or tenth military school he hitchhiked to Mexico City, a tall, gangling sixteen-year-old. He stayed down there two years, got into some kind of trouble with the city government and returned to New Orleans on a shrimp boat.

In Mexico City he learned to hate the refined forms of work only slightly more than he hated physical labor. He returned to Sunpark, managed to blackmail his father into paying him three thousand a year just to live away from the house. He went to the university, flunked out, returned home to find his father now refusing to aid him at all. He needed a lot of money for liquor, transient girls and new clothes. Whatever he got now he collected in niggardly amounts from his mother.

He said now, giggling a little, "I hear all over town that you were around asking about me. They thought you were an investigator from the credit bureau."

"I wanted to find out something about you."

"Did you?"

"I found out you're a first-class son of a bitch."

"Hell, I'm just sorry you went to so much trouble."

"Well now I know."

"Yes, but, ole buddy, I could have told you anything you wanted to know. Been pleased to do it."

I got an okay from the control tower at Sunpark and put the Cessna down. I taxied to the hangar and for a moment glued my gaze on that sign and Jimmy Clark's smiling face. I felt my stomach muscles constrict.

"Wait'll I pay Clark for this flight," Coates said. "I'll buy you a drink. We got to keep this looking like flying lessons."

I nodded and he strode into the hangar with that crazy loose-gaited walk that made him look as if his mother had been frightened in pregnancy by a rag doll. I shrugged out of my leather jacket and stood in the shadow of Clark's sign, waiting for him.

He opened the door to Clark's office and then stepped back. Judy passed him, coming out of there.

My heart went into a tailspin. It made me physically ill to see her now with what I had on my conscience. I turned quickly as if I were checking the Cessna, hoping she wouldn't come near me.

My luck is all bad. I heard her heels on the cement. I could smell her, I could feel her nearness.

"Hi."

I turned. I didn't try to smile. I hadn't seen her for almost a week—an eternity.

I jerked my head toward Clark's office. "You mean you and your mother haven't disinherited that character yet?"

She smiled, reached out to touch my arm. I took one step back. This put the sun in my face. I didn't move. My eyes burned anyhow.

"You were with that odd-looking character," Judy said. "I thought you told me you didn't know him."

"I don't. I teach him to fly. I teach all Clark's pupils to fly. If I didn't, he'd teach them himself and they'd kill themselves even quicker."

"I wish you didn't hate Jimmy so terribly." There was an odd look in her face.

"I wish I didn't too," I said. "But we might as well face it. He turns it to clabber. He affects everybody but you and your mother that way."

"Why, Buz, that isn't true. He's well-liked. Respected."

"Has he been telling you this?"

She giggled in spite of herself. She glanced over her shoulder. "I don't like your friend, Buz. I wish you'd stay away from him."

"How about that? If we don't have something to fight about, we make up something."

"I'm sorry, Buz. I'm only thinking about you."

"I think about you—but that gets me nowhere, either."

Her face flushed. "That's your fault, Buz. Once I'd have married you in two minutes. I wouldn't even listen to what Jimmy told me. But—no. Would you still love me when I was the only gray-haired stewardess in the business?"

My voice matched hers. "It won't be that way. Give me a chance, Judy. Give me a chance."

She frowned, staring into my eyes. I pulled my gaze away. Her voice was very low as if she were frightened and didn't know what made her afraid. "Be careful, Buz. You hear? Don't be a fool. Please don't be a fool."

Chapter Ten

I didn't sleep that night and got out of bed the next morning before six. Coates and I were up until three A.M. going over our plan, going over the town of Fort Dale until we knew it better than its mayor. We found out how long it would take us to stroll, casually and apparently even a little intoxicated, a half-mile. We discussed endlessly how we could nullify the effectiveness of the Fort Dale sheriff and constable. We hit on a lot of plans, and settled on the simplest; somehow we would get arrested and in a police car. We decided how long we would have to be in the bank. Surprise was going to work for us; we could count on getting in and out of there under ten minutes. I went over everything with him until he slapped his hands over his ears at the sound of my voice. The whole operation had to have a casualness about it. Part of it we would have to play by ear, but I left no more to chance than I had to.

There was a knock on the door a little after seven. I

answered it, knotting my tie. Clark insisted that we look neat on the job; it imparted confidence to the suckers.

I opened the door. Coates stood there, giving me his loose-lipped version of a grin. He carried three large bundles.

He stepped inside and slapped the door closed behind him. He was hopped-up on excitement. It acted upon him like a needle or smoke.

He threw the packages on the bed and began ripping them open. He tossed me a pair of tan overalls, the type mechanics wear around grease racks, with zipper from crotch to throat.

"Saleswoman had a fit when I bought a pair your size," he said. "I told her I was buying them for my little boy. Hope they fit, Sonny."

He held the pair of coveralls he'd bought for himself up against his body. He turned on his heel and toe, like a model. His laugh was a fluting sound. "What the well-dressed young fortune hunters will wear."

"Keep your voice down."

"Hell, what difference does it make?"

"I don't know. Did you get the rest of the stuff?"

"You gave me the list, Mother, and I went shopping. Two cheap suitcases." He unwrapped two cardboard bags. "Even the cheapest ones are expensive," he said.

I scowled at him because I'd warned him a dozen times about buying anything that could be traced.

He spoke quickly. "Oh, come on now, Little Mother, you worry too much. I bought these two cases at a drugstore. They had ninety of them, and these were the cheapest they had."

I grunted. The whole thing might be a laugh to laughing boy, but I wanted nothing that could be easily traced.

I opened one of the suitcases, folded my coveralls and stored them in it. Coates opened another package and handed me a woman's silk stocking. He kept its mate. He unsnapped the other bag and tossed his coveralls and stocking into it. Then he gave me a pair of dark glasses and kept a pair for himself. I checked my mental list and that was everything, except one item.

"Cloth bags," I said. "Did you get 'em?"

47

He tried to sound offended. "Man, you got to start trusting me."

"Why?"

He shrugged as though providing a reason beat him. He shook out half a dozen five-pound cloth bags. The excitement inside him made him shiver suddenly, just looking at those bags. He could already see them stuffed with loot. "You think this will be enough?"

He had brought a morning newspaper. I unfolded it and checked the weather news. It looked good to me. The barometer was dropping, a thundershower was forecast for early afternoon.

"Coates," I said, "what you got against pulling the deal today?"

He stared at me and his hands shook visibly. "Today? Just like that? Man, are you joking?"

"I never joke about money," I told him. I showed him the weather forecast. "We move with the weather. Right? That's all we've been waiting for. Today looks fine."

"Boy," he said. "Boy." He walked around the room, bumping a chair, his arms swinging. "I've thought about it for a hell of a time—and all of a sudden you say, right now." He swallowed and thrust his hands into his coat pockets. He brought out two automatics. "Pawnshop stuff," he said. "I had to sign for them. I forget what name I signed."

I took one of the guns. He pulled ammo clips from another pocket. His face was white. My own insides were beginning to act up.

We put the guns in the suitcases, checked everything. "We can't carry these suitcases to the hangar. Nosy Jimmy Clark would find some reason to inspect them," I said. "So what we'll do is, you go over to the Island Airport, give me time to get out to International. Then you call Clark and tell him you're at Island and want me to come over and pick you up for a lesson. You can have all this stuff with you and nobody over there will think anything about it."

He grinned. "What you are, Buz, is a genius."

It was almost nine when I arrived at the airport. I rode the bus out there and it didn't bother me at all this morning. I walked through the administration building and headed toward hangar row. I could look at Jimmy Clark's sign this morning without my usual morning sickness.

I saw that Jimmy was in his office. I didn't want to talk to him so I waved my leather jacket in salute when he glanced up through the glass partitions. Even at that distance the look of smugness around his mouth pained me. I didn't see how Judy and her mother tolerated him in the house.

I called a mechanic and he and I pushed the Cessna out to the runway. I could have rolled the job out there alone, but it would have struck off-key for Jimmy. Buz Johnson never exerted himself, and I wanted this morning to look like every other morning.

I opened the cabin doorway and was climbing in when Jimmy came bounding through his office door.

"What gives?" he yelled. He loved to chew people out before an audience. "Where you think you're going?"

"Nowhere. Just wanted to warm it." I waited, sure now that Coates hadn't put through the call yet from Island Airport.

"You buying the gas now, Ace? Why don't you wait for a student? You can't warm it up while you explain the controls to them any more?"

I looked at him standing with his hair red and his face red. I shrugged. "No. I don't explain anything to them. Your pupils just want to fly, Clark. They don't care why, or how they do it."

"Don't be wasting my money, Ace. Get out of that plane."

I felt chilled with the knot of anger that iced up my belly but I swung out of the plane. I wanted to hear that engine fire. I wanted to listen to it before Coates and I took off in it. If there were any bugs, the greasemonkeys could pinch them out now.

I walked into his office with him. He went behind his desk, glanced at a new photo of Judy on it and then sat down. I didn't look at the picture. He wanted me to look at it and bleed. I could bleed without looking at it.

He went to work on some papers and I leaned back, trying to keep my eyes off that telephone. The minutes dragged. What was the matter with Coates? It was nearer to the Island Airport from my place than to International. I had ridden a city bus out here and Coates had driven his own car.

I could hear Clark's pen scratching as he worked. I could hear the rapid, irregular thudding of my own heart. It got so I could not keep my gaze off that telephone. It seemed as dead as though the electric current had been taken from it.

I felt the slow bulge of sweat globules on my forehead; my shirt got damp at my armpits. The partition walls seemed to crowd in on me. I began to need a drink, and I had not thought about a drink all morning. I wiped my palm downward across my mouth.

Finally, when it was almost ten o'clock, Clark glanced up at me across his desk. There was something in his face I could not understand. He seemed to be laughing, and yet the brand of contempt in his eyes was new even to him.

"Oh, by the way," he said. "About ten minutes before you got here, your student-pal Sid Coates telephoned. Wanted a flying lesson this morning."

"Hell, why didn't you tell me?"

Clark went on smiling. "Why should I? He wanted a lesson, he could come out here."

"Where was he?"

"Out at Island Airport for Christ's sake."

"What's wrong with that? His money is as good as anybody else's, isn't it?"

Clark shrugged. "Yeah. But no better. Sounded to me like he was drunk."

"So?" I had a mental picture of Coates, hopped-up with excitement, trying to keep his voice level as he talked with Clark. "You riding herd on student morals now?"

"No. But it sounded to me like he was out there, got drunk, and wanted taxi service."

"What the hell? As long as he pays you."

"Man, what's got you cobbed off? What do you care? I told Coates we didn't run a taxi service. If he wants lessons, he can make arrangements in advance, like the rest of my students do. I told him that, too."

I didn't move. My shirt felt soggy wet. I didn't like what I saw in Clark's phony-smiling face. I told myself it was just my conscience. But my hands were shaking. I needed a drink. I walked out of there, went over to the Rudder and got one.

"There's just one thing I want you to keep in your mind," Coates said.

He was prancing back and forth in my room that same night. It had started to rain at noon, steadily and yet not enough to make flying impractical. It had rained all afternoon, the perfect kind of rough weather we wanted for our little mission. Only it hadn't gotten off the ground. Coates was sick about it. I didn't blame him. I felt ill, too, but illness with Coates was a ridiculous thing. He couldn't stand being indisposed without ascertaining that everybody in earshot knew about it.

"Your friend Jimmy Clark is suspicious," he said. "I could sense that on the telephone. I could tell the way he talked to me. It was almost as if he knew what we were planning and he was laughing at us because we were helpless without that stinking plane of his. Oh, you can say what you want to, but that boy suspects something."

"He's no friend of mine," I said.

He stopped pacing. "What kind of funny crack is that supposed to be?"

"You said I could say what I wanted. I just wanted you to know Clark is no friend of mine."

"Very funny. A guy like that can get us in one hell of a lot of trouble."

"Not if you keep your head." I walked to the window. The rain had stopped but the street was still wet, with night lights reflected in it. "It's not as though we plan to use his plane on the job. Like I said, we'll steal another two-place and then exchange it for another. Even the time it takes won't matter as long as we're not more than half an hour in Fort Dale. It'll cover our tracks, and it'll take any heat off Jimmy Clark."

"Sounds fine. But he's still suspicious."

"I admit that this morning I was afraid something had happened and Clark had stumbled on what we wanted. But I thought it over. First I worried, like you are worrying. Then I started thinking—the way you're not. How in hell, I asked myself, could he suspect anything? You know what was the matter with him this morning?"

51

"He knew we each wanted that plane."

"No. He knew you wanted it. You see, you never signed on with him. You let me take you up for lessons and then you go pay him for one lesson. This doesn't make Clark feel like a big man. If he doesn't feel like a big man, he gets ill. So then he has to prove to you what a big man he is. That's what he was doing this morning."

"Oh, that boy is sick."

"Just the same, we have to consider him now, along with the weather."

"My God. Something else."

"There'll be plenty of other things before we're through. If we just keep ahead of them, we're all right. Look, you might as well get one thing straight. I hate Clark's guts, but I'll grovel for him until I get my hands on that money."

"Okay, Buz. I'll buy that."

"Good. We'll get our turn. We'll rub his face in it. But not right now. Tomorrow I want you to show up at his place and sign on for regular lessons."

He paced a moment, chewing this over. I saw what was wrong with it before he did, but after a moment, Coates said, "That allays the old boy's suspicions, but how does it help us? We can't choose weather like today, the kind we want, Buz, and work it into a schedule that will please that louse."

"I'm pleased to see you've started thinking and stopped worrying."

"Don't fool yourself. I haven't stopped worrying. So how do we get the kind of day we want and the lesson-time we want?"

"We'll have to wait until they match."

"My God, Buz. We can't do that. I can't wait. Not now when we almost pulled the thing off today. We don't know when another right day will come along."

"We'll take the best we can. That's all we can do."

He wiped the back of his hand across his mouth. "I don't like it, Buz. It's like something is going wrong already before we get in the sky."

Somebody knocked on the door. We went tense and stared at each other as though we were thieves, or two kids caught smoking in the bathroom.

"You're leaving," I said. "You were just leaving no matter who it is." I said it under my breath. I waited only to see that Coates understood. He nodded. I pushed the two suitcases under my bed. Then I got up, batted the wrinkles out of my trouser knees and went to the door.

I opened it. There stood Judy.

Coates was at my elbow, hat in hand. He tried to grin. He looked ill.

"Hi," he said to her and went out into the hall. He didn't wait to be introduced.

I heard Judy's sharp intake of breath. It was like spoken disapproval, but she nodded at Coates and entered the room. I closed the door.

For a moment neither of us spoke. I saw her shoulders quiver slightly. "Every time I see you, Buz, he's around somewhere. It gives me the creeps."

"I'm studying him for the interplanetary committee."

She frowned. "You're mighty cool about all this."

I felt my face growing warm. "About what? I'm a big boy. I can have some friends. You act as though something was wrong."

"Isn't something wrong, Buz?"

I went close to her, put my arms around her. I pulled her hard against me and felt her warm tears against my cheek. I don't know why the heat of her tears chilled me all the way through.

"How could anything be wrong?" I said. "You're here. With me."

"Yes. I'm here."

My hands moved on her. She pulled away from me. "Don't touch me, Buz."

"Why not?"

"I don't want you to."

"Why not?"

"Please, Buz. This doesn't get us anywhere."

"Is this the way you treat your pilot up in New York?" All right, so I hated myself for saying it, but that didn't change anything. I couldn't help saying it.

She looked as if I had hit her across the face. "What about Johnny?"

"Johnny? Is that his name?"

"I thought you knew."

"What makes him so different?"

"Security, hope for a future. He's very good. You'd like him."

"Oh, I'm sure of it." I moved away from her. "It doesn't matter. I've had it, as far as you're concerned."

"I'll always love you, Buz."

I shook my head. "When a woman worries about security while you've got her in your arms, run don't walk." My laugh had a bitter sound, even more bitter than I intended. "Once upon a time you didn't talk security when I loved you."

"I didn't talk about it—as long as there was any hope for it."

"Oh, for God's sake. What did you come around here for? What did you want?"

"I don't know. I truly don't know. I'm on a flight to New York tonight. I thought—I thought you might ride out to the airport with me."

"Sure," I said. "Why not? We can chat all the way out there about Johnny."

Her chin tilted and something happened in her eyes. She did not speak for a moment. Then she said, softly, "You're so wrong, Buz. About everything. That's what hurts so badly."

She glanced toward the door. She didn't say anything but we both knew she was thinking about Sid Coates. I did not speak either. Whatever she had come here to say, she had changed her mind and she wasn't going to say it. I found a tie, draped it around my neck, shrugged into a sport jacket and we got out of there. She had her taxi waiting at the curb downstairs.

She was crying softly when we got out of the cab at Eastern's terminal building entrance. She acted as if this were her last flight, as if she were never going to see me again, or as though I'd said something that hurt too deeply to discuss. I could not think what either of us had said on the ride out to make her cry. Maybe the way things were with us, neither of us had to say anything any more to make the other cry. The tears were brimming right there behind our eyes, waiting. When things get hopeless enough, you don't have anything left but tears. And then sometimes to keep from shedding them, you strike out and hurt your love so that she will shed your tears for you.

Jimmy Clark was standing just outside the glass doors as if he had been standing there a long time. He looked very dapper, with shoes shined, suit pressed, hair newly trimmed. He looked very successful. It was hard to believe we toiled in the same operation. The only thing that pleased me was that Jimmy could not even force a smile. That phony grin had come unglued and fallen off his pan.

He came forward, noticed instantly that Judy had been crying. His fists knotted and he glared at me. "Why don't you stay away from my daughter?"

"Why don't you?"

Judy touched his arm. "It's all right, Jimmy."

"He's nothing but trouble to you, baby. He always has been." He ignored me then, as though I'd ceased to exist. "I thought I was going to drive you out here, Judy."

I'm sorry, Jim. I came in a cab." She sighed. "I was afraid you might be tied up."

"I got home early, Judy. Very early." His voice was cold.

I laughed. "I work for him. That's what makes him think he can talk to me like this," I said. "What's your excuse, Judy?"

She glanced at me, shook her head. "I'm sorry, Jim. I wanted to talk with Buz. Something I—wanted to tell him."

Jimmy's phony smile showed again, and for some reason that escaped me, he seemed relieved.

"I'm sorry," Judy said. "I must go. I'll be late."

She brushed his cheek with a daughterly kiss. Then she turned and looked at me. Everybody in the terminal building knew she kissed me—long and lingeringly—though she did not come near me at all. She walked away quickly and didn't look my way again.

I sat down at the bar in the Rudder Room. The saloon was crowded at this hour. Waitresses glided through the vaguely lighted areas as if on skates, bartenders were fluid behind the bar. For me the whole world was a drab and empty void. I ordered a drink but before I could get it, someone touched my shoulder. I glanced around. It was Jimmy Clark.

"Get lost," I said.

"Buz, I want to talk to you." He jerked his head toward a small table for two, hard against the floor-to-ceiling glass overlooking the runways.

"Get lost."

"Please, Buz."

The tone of his voice, and the word which was so new to him that he stumbled over it got me; this and the sense of wrong that would not leave me now. I spoke to the bartender and moved with Clark to the table. Below us on the field, men were loading the underbellies of planes, a gasoline truck was gassing up a DC-6. Men were running around down there and you could see the way they bent forward that the wind was high. The wind was high up here, too. It was about to hurtle me off the face of the earth.

"The drinks are on me, Buz."

"Sure they are."

We ordered and the waitress went away. I didn't say anything. He wanted this confab. I wasn't worried about making it easy for him.

His voice was almost humanely considerate, and that was really something for this boy. He said, "First, Judy asked me to tell you something."

"Oh?"

"Just before she went on duty. I thought she had told you. It seems—according to her—she couldn't."

"What's the mystery?"

"Maybe I can tell you why Judy came by your place tonight."

"Maybe I can tell *you*," I said.

He shook his head. "No. I don't think you can. I think you would be wrong no matter what you said. She'd already told me the news, and said she had to tell you. But I guess she lost her nerve. Couldn't stand to hurt you or something."

"But you have no such compunctions?"

"No."

My throat constricted. The lights of the dim room flared brightly and blinded me with their brilliance.

"Judy is going to be married, Johnson. This is her last flight. She's marrying this nice young fellow in New York.

That's what she came by to tell you, whether she told you or not."

"Ahhh," I said. It was an agonized sound.

He glanced around, phony smile pasted on his face. He said, "I've mentioned him. They're in love. He's coming here for the marriage ceremony. I hope you'll be decent enough to keep out of the way."

"Skeleton in the closet, eh?"

"Judy has no past any of us are trying to conceal, of course. But you are a mistake she made."

"She tell you that?"

"Nobody had to tell me."

"What a son of a bitch you are."

"Keep your voice down."

I pressed my hand against my mouth. He was spinning around in front of me, a phony smile on a whirling cord.

"You ought to be happy, Jimmy. You've done everything you could to smash us up."

"I didn't have to do anything. You did it all."

"You helped it along." He finished off his drink, signaled for the check. His smile flattened out on his face now.

"I just thought you ought to know," he said. He paid the check to the exact penny minus a tip and then he walked out.

I don't know how I got home. I didn't know then, I never knew afterward. I was sitting at that little knee-rubbing table in the Rudder Room, staring out over the darkened field, and the next thing I knew I was standing in front of the wall mirror that hung in my apartment and staring at something white and rutted and agonized, a shapeless face in that glass. It looked wild and strange and unreal.

It took me a long time to realize it was my own face.

I stood there, my shoulders hunched forward and studied that Hallowe'en mask in that mirror. I couldn't pull my gaze from the ugly face in the glass. My frustrated, stark, bloodless, hated face.

I endured it as long as I could. I felt my fist knotting at my side, felt my muscles bunching all the way up my arm to my shoulder.

I smashed my fist into the exact center of that glass. The

57

frame rocked against the wall and the wall shook. But the important thing was what happened to that face. It was gone. It had smashed into parts and bits like jigs in a puzzle, and the glass was spidery like a web and it no longer reflected my ugly face as a whole. . . .

I walked away stiffly, moving around the room and making animal sounds in my throat. Something snagged my attention and I stopped, staring at a picture hanging on the wall. When I moved past, it reflected my face. I could not stand that. I drove my fist into it and the wall rattled again and glass shards spilled slowly from the frame and I did not look at it again.

Ahead I saw another picture. I smashed my fist into it, feeling the sharp bite of pain where pieces of glass drove into my knuckles and between my fingers. I moaned aloud but not because of the pain. I didn't feel the pain, and when I noticed the blood flicking from my fist I didn't care about that either. All I knew was that there was another glass-framed picture and I broke it, and that was not enough so I broke everything I could lift and hurl in the room, and my fist bled and it spilled blood but I did not look at my fist.

I walked rigidly around the room looking for something else to smash and there was nothing more. My mouth spewed sounds and I wasn't even aware of what I was saying. There were no more pictures, no more mirrors, no more bottles, but there was a window overlooking the street and I listed toward it as fast as I could walk and drove my fist through it.

By now people were banging at my door. I didn't even bother telling them to go away.

She was marrying a guy named Johnny. A pilot she met in New York. Why? I knew what she would have told me, but she couldn't tell me, even when she wanted to. This guy offered her security and I yelled at her now, how long you think you're going to be able to stand that, for Christ's sake?

I went on yelling. You can't leave me, Judy. God damn it, you can't leave me. What will I do without you? I know what it is without you when I believed I'd some day have you, and I can't stand it when I know I never will have you now. I can't take that. I got to have something. There's nobody else. There never was. What do I have to do to prove it, for Christ's sake? What do I have to do? Why didn't you tell me? But we had ridden all the way to the airport and you didn't tell me, you couldn't force yourself to tell me, and Jimmy Clark had to tell me.

An agonized sound pressed through my throat, and I cried out as you might in a nightmare that you can no longer endure. I stood there with my hand bleeding, people banging at my door. I looked around for something else to smash, but there wasn't anything left to break.

Chapter Eleven

The newspaper weather report forecast rain with clouds, overcast skies. I had waited almost a week for this, a week in which I'd existed inside a ball of hatred.

I was in Clark's office when I read the afternoon weather chart for Friday. I balled the paper in my fist, tossed it toward the wastebasket. I had waited long enough. This was close to what I wanted, and even if it were not reliable because it reached ahead more than eleven hours, I decided to gamble on it.

The truth was, I couldn't sit around like this any more. "Clark," I said. Jimmy looked up from behind his desk and gave me his meaningless smile. We hadn't said much to each other in the week since our little chat in the Rudder Room. "Sid Coates wanted me to ask you if he could charter your plane for a flight down the coast to Verona City tomorrow."

Clark frowned. "Verona City?"

"Yeah. That's right."

"All day?"

"Most of it."

"That'll cost him a wad of dough."

"What the hell? His mother can afford it."

Jimmy laughed with contempt. "You two guys are a real pair."

I grunted.

"Why didn't he ask me himself?" Clark asked.

"Last time he made a request of you, you turned him down. He wants to fly to Verona City to see some guy. And it'll give him a chance to log some air time."

"All day?" Clark said again. A smile that was odd, even for Jimmy Clark, began to spread over his face. "And he wants you to go along with him, eh?"

"I'm his instructor, remember?"

This twisted smile broadened. Maybe it was only my own conscience, maybe it was the tamped-down hatred I felt for him, but I would have sworn Clark was suspicious. He even looked as if he *knew* why we wanted to use his plane.

He got up and paced back and forth behind his desk. He seemed about to speak a couple of times, and his Billy Graham-type evangelistic scowl was worse than a smile. Once he stood there and stared at me for a few seconds. Finally he shook his head slightly and agreed.

"Sure. You guys take it." He laughed. "Why not?"

I stayed downtown until two A.M. the next morning waiting for the Friday papers to hit the street. I couldn't have slept anyway and even though I had permission to use Clark's Cessna, I wanted the latest possible weather bureau report on those promised overcast skies.

I bought a paper and walked with it folded under my arm. I didn't open it until I got inside my apartment. This was a superstition with me. The longer I delayed, the better the news was going to be.

I poured a glass of orange juice, sat down at the table and thumbed through the paper until I found the weather report. My hand was still sore and stiff from the glass slivers.

I laughed aloud.

The weather news couldn't have been more perfect if they'd served it up for me personally. I read it over three times before I convinced myself that there wasn't some error.

I picked up the telephone, dialed Sid's number. The bell jangled for a long time in his apartment. Finally he answered, his voice sleep-drugged.

"Sid."

"My God, Buz. Three o'clock. I just got to sleep."

"Wake up. This is it."

"You nuts? This time of night?"

"I'll be by your place in a taxi in about forty minutes. It'll take us maybe twenty minutes more to ride out to the airport. I think we ought to be airborne by daylight."

"Buz, you're having a nightmare."

"Am I? Listen." I read the weather report to him. Even across the wires I could sense the tension start in him, winding him up. "Cold front moving south. Warm front moving north. Precipitation. Barometer falling. Rough winds. Rainfall heavy by afternoon. Overcast skies. You know what this means, Sid, for sure? It means no light craft in the air."

He'd caught fire by now. He was wide awake. He laughed. "None except ours, baby." Then his voice dropped. "How we going to get the plane? Tomorrow isn't my day to fly. Clark won't let me rent the Cessna."

"He's already agreed," I told him. "You're hiring me and the Cessna for a flight to Verona City. Visit that friend of yours down there. That's as much in the opposite direction from Fort Dale as I could get without ending in the Gulf."

"Sounds fine."

"He's really going to gouge you on plane rental."

He laughed. "The hell with costs, son. Don't even think about such trifles."

A sort of drugged sleeplessness possessed the Sunpark International at five A.M. We got out of the cab at the administration building. Fluorescent, neon and curb lights cast an unearthly glow against the deepening dark. The baggage boys lolled on benches against the walls, awake but too nearly asleep to get to their feet when a cab reached the curb. Inside the white, lighted corridors, flight-desk clerks stared fixedly at papers before them, never moving. Nobody was actually asleep out here, but they weren't truly awake, either.

Sid and I stood on the curb at American's entrance. Sid paid the driver and we watched the cab move away in the darkness. The taillight winked when he stopped for the highway, and I felt so good that I winked back in the darkness.

"What about these damned suitcases," Sid said. "Somebody will remember we had them."

"Hell with them. Nobody at Fort Dale will ever see these suitcases. Everybody carries suitcases at an airport. You'd look half-dressed without one."

He loped along behind me through the administration building. People were slouched in the leather chairs asleep or dozing, jerking up their heads every time the p.a. system came to life. We went out on the ramp, walking against the wind, toward Hangar 2.

Sid belched. "Ulcers," he said. "I'll feel better when we're in the air."

"You chicken?"

"Hell no. I always belch when I'm awake this time of the day."

I grinned at him over my shoulder. "Son, we're in luck. We haven't even seen anybody we know yet."

"The tower is going to know we left here—and when."

"Man. No wonder you got ulcers."

The fact that people would know we took off from International before daybreak didn't worry me. I had been living in a void for the past week, hypnotized against thinking about Judy. If I allowed myself a thought, I kept it on the flight Sid and I were going to make, and how I could work out any rough angles. Sometimes when I had three or four whiskys-with-beer at the Old Sarge's Bar, I would even smile to myself a little. I couldn't share my secret with anybody, but when I was half-stewed, I realized that Sid and I were like Robin Hood—only we had pawnshop guns instead of bow and arrow. We were like Jesse James, only we were going to fly in like men from Mars instead of making the take on horseback. Modern Jesse James. Ultramodern Robin Hood.

And these were the only thoughts I had allowed myself. I kept away from Judy when she returned to town, away from Jimmy Clark as much as possible. My room was repaired and I forgot that too, consciously. I heard that Judy's young pilot was due in town, or perhaps had arrived; I didn't listen that closely.

But when I had a share of a hundred grand, I would be different, everything would be different. Having this one fact to cling to made it possible for me to work with Jimmy Clark and not get thrown in jail for assault.

I hurried a little now, going ahead of Sid into the hangar. The suitcase banged against my leg, and the slight pain was pleasant. It seemed to me that the way things were going I ought to win out. Everything was flying along, smooth and easy, increasingly fast, like something caught in a wind tunnel where nothing could stop it or turn it back, but nothing could interfere with its perfect progress, either.

I opened the door of the cabin plane, stowed my suitcase behind the seats, watched Sid put his away. Everything seemed to be on our side. There was no airport near Fort Dale, and this in itself insured success: no airport, no pursuit. I made a little song of it in my mind, humming. And even if there had been an airport, the weather today was foul enough to ground all light craft. Sid and I would have the skies to ourselves.

I tried to decide what color Cadillac I would drive. It would be a convertible, of course. I like to ride with the top down. I laughed aloud, but Sid didn't even hear me. He was busy talking to himself.

The engine coughed and spit and came to life. I let it warm up inside the hangar because I didn't want to attract too much attention out on the sky chutes.

We rolled it outside. I contacted the tower, got clearance, wind direction and velocity. The radio man sounded astounded. "Buz, is that you, Buz? I never knew you were sober enough to fly this time of the day."

I cursed to myself because this guy knew me, but it was not important. I sweated it a little, but managed to chuckle and assure him that I wouldn't fly in the same plane with myself if I were sober.

We taxied along the runway, revved the motor and headed into the wind. I put the Cessna in the air, climbing, and the next thing I did was to kill radio contact with the control tower.

I glanced at my watch, feeling the sweet taste of excitement in my throat and bubbling up into the back of my mouth. It was 5:45 A.M. and we were airborne.

"This gives us plenty of time to steal a plane in the dark and set Clark's down on the strip at Berry Town." I said it aloud, but was speaking mostly to myself.

"Man, you do worry about hiding his plane!"

"It's not Clark I'm worrying about. But if he's mixed up in it, Judy will be. I don't want to hurt her."

"Sir Galahad."

"The hell with that. I'm Robin Hood."

I glanced back at the receding airfield and grinned. I hadn't felt this good since Korea. I knew how Jesse James felt. I knew how Robin Hood felt. And better than that, I knew how I felt.

I felt like the man from Mars.

Then, without warning, this faint sense of wrong began nagging at me. For a moment I didn't realize what it was. Then I knew. The sun was suddenly up, all around us. Daybreak is sudden and complete in this flat country, and I had forgotten that. The sun was like a bright yellow egg yolk behind us. It already glittered in the bay below. And there was no sign of that cold front with rough winds, beaucoup rain.

"What's wrong?" Sid said.

"You see any signs of rain?" I glanced at him. He'd been sitting rigidly since we left the ground, hands locked in his lap and face taut with almost unbearable tensions.

He moved his head stiffly, scanning the horizon. "It's early yet," he said. Then: "You sure you read that paper right, Buz?"

"I read it right. A half-dozen times. Don't worry, those thunderheads will move right down on us. When the warm front strikes the cold front, we got it made. I've had them too many times when I didn't want them for them to fail me now."

"Well. Here we are," Sid said.

"A couple of rich guys."

"Fortune hunters. Take gold from the rich cattle farmers who don't know how to appreciate it and give it to the poor fliers who need so much."

"It's a mission." Sid laughed. "A crusade."

Sid turned and took a fifth of Echo Springs from his suitcase.

"What you want with that thing?" I said.

"Got another one. One for you."

"Hell."

"Case of snake bite."

"Sid, don't be a damned fool. Don't start drinking now." Coates laughed and removed the cap. He drank the first long pull thirstily, smacked his lips. "You run the plane. I'll do my part."

I felt a sudden burst of rage. "Just be sure you can," I told him.

Down inside me, the feeling persisted that here was something I hadn't anticipated, something I should have checked out but hadn't checked out. Sid was my partner in this thing. I had investigated his past but forgotten his present. This robbery was a gamble that called for strictly sober thinking. We'd planned a drunk act in Fort Dale, but I had intended it to be all pretense. But there was no sense in telling Coates not to drink, because . . .

The truth hit me like a fist in the nose. This is what I had done to all those guys who had depended on me to fly their planes. I had drunked out, goofed off—and now I was getting it all back. Coates was a lush. That's what he had become, a real lush, and he needed this stuff for a crutch. This robbery was all his idea. But he wasn't going to be able to execute it without a bottle to nurse on.

Welcome aboard, partner.

I suddenly hated him, as the guys I'd once flown for must have hated me when I failed them. I felt superior to Coates now; not better, just different. I needed whisky so I could endure living among people on the ground. I needed whisky so I could live with myself while I accomplished nothing. But when I had a goal, a chance to do something, to go somewhere, I had all the excitement I needed and a bottle didn't interest me. I even wondered: if I get down there to South America with Greenie and I'm busy thirty hours a day with problems that have to be sweated out, will I . . . And then I shook that out of my mind.

I glanced at Coates gulping down the straight whisky and I laughed a little to myself. Partner, I thought.

Hail, partner.

Clark was right about Sid and me. We made a great pair.

65

Chapter Twelve

I followed the black lane of the causeway west across Sun Bay. Only a few cars used the bridges and approaches at this hour. From up here the bay was a dark tongue of water licking between the mangrove swamps and the dredged fills, flat and white, like desert sand and growing nothing but low-priced subdivisions. Far ahead, the strip of peninsula between bay and gulf was laid out in orderly streets stacked tightly with retirement homes and trailer parks. Beyond this was a strip of courtesy islands and the flat green gulf. I looked for thunderheads out on that horizon. I saw none.

I circled over the small airport inside the city limits of Bay City. It was six A.M. I had hoped to make it earlier, but I saw no movement down there and felt better. With even the beginnings of the promised overcast, none of the Sunday fliers would think of flying their planes this morning. Would they risk it now, in bright and sunny skies? Maybe not. I had believed the weather forecast, hadn't I? Well, then, a lot of the other fliers should be influenced by it, and stay grounded.

I had to hope for that.

I laughed to myself, looking down at the neat rows of private planes lined up like sitting ducks beside the runways, the single hangar and the field office sitting forlorn and quiet a city block from the last two-place.

"What you laughing at?" Coates asked.

"I'm pleased with myself, friend. I'm a genius, and I never realized it any more than when I see things working smoothly just as I said they would."

"You sure hell didn't get the weather you ordered."

"You can't have everything."

"Without that, we got nothing."

"You're clucking, chicken."

He took a pull on the bottle, frowned down at the parked planes. "Which one of those babies you want?"

I shook my head, putting the nose of the Cessna into a long silent glide into a runway.

"It doesn't matter which plane I want. It's the plane we got to take, the job that's farthest away from the field office. The less attention we attract right now, the better."

I couldn't help smiling to myself, thinking how clever this thing was. We picked up a plane here and when we flew out of Fort Dale, the plane that the state police would report would have no connection with the silver Cessna job that Coates and I had borrowed for a training flight south to Verona City.

I let the Cessna roll to within a few feet of the two-place job at the end of the line of privately owned sports jobs.

"You want me to take it up?" Coates said.

"No. You keep this baby running. But remember this—something might go wrong." I glanced toward the field office. There was still no sign of activity over there even though we were on the ground, motor idling.

"What could go wrong?" Sid wanted to know.

"Maybe nothing. But you stay on the ground until I'm in the air. I'm not about to have you take off and leave me grounded."

Sid laughed and took over the controls of the Cessna. "I'll follow you up, baby, like a mama eagle."

He took one more long pull at the bottle.

"Watch that stuff, too," I told him. I stepped out on the ground, flexing my muscles, watching the field office and the half-closed hangar.

I sauntered around the Cessna, keeping it as casual as I could. I wanted it to appear from the distance that our cabin plane might have developed some minor defect and I was out kicking tires like a used-car customer.

I took another quick half-glance at the field office. The whole field was flat and deserted, still slightly damp early in the morning. The sun glistened like tiny lights in dew. When I was between the Cessna and the larger job, I ran a little, swung into the cockpit. I set controls, pressed the starter, waiting without breathing. A strange plane didn't worry me. I knew them from jennies to jets. This plane rated with the Cessna, with perhaps slightly more horsepower.

The engine growled, sputtered, almost turned over, but spat instead. I felt the sweat break out on my forehead. This couldn't happen to me. Damned if I was going to be balked by a Sunday afternoon crate.

I jerked my head around, still pressing the starter. Coates was framed in the window of the Cessna, like a tableau of fear, like something done by Dali. His face was stark, whiter than his eyebrows. He was begging without words for me to tell him what was wrong.

And I didn't know.

Suddenly Coates yelled at me. "Buz!"

My face was filmed with sweat by now. I studied that instrument panel and everything checked out, gas, oil, everything.

But all I got was that whine, the increasing growl until it almost caught. But it didn't catch. It spit at me instead, almost as if it were emitting some kind of mechanical laughter.

"Buz!"

"What you want?"

He waved an arm, pointing toward the hangar. "Forget that damned plane. Let's get out of here. Look over there. One of those greasemonkeys has spotted you!"

Frustration knotted inside me. I kept my gaze fixed on that mechanic. He came out of the hangar, stared down the runway toward us. For a moment he couldn't make up his mind, and then probably because the Cessna was a stranger to him, he decided against us. He ran along the cement, yelling. He was too far away for me to hear what he was saying and I didn't care anyway. I gave that starter one last nudge, got nothing.

I ducked down, slid out of the plane and ran across to the Cessna. I leaped and scrambled inside. Coates had the plane in motion as I slammed the door and secured the catch.

We were going upward into the wind as we passed the mechanic. He yelled something at us but this boy just wasn't getting through. I lifted my arm and waved at him.

He gawked after us, and then he waved back.

When we were airborne, Coates turned the plane inland. The sun was rising now, a white-hot morning ball.

"What now?" Coates said.

I was still sweating, and swearing inwardly. I had been stopped by a sportman's play toy, a ground-hopper's pogo-stick.

I grabbed the bottle of Echo Springs. I held it for a moment thinking how badly I needed a drink.

I didn't answer Coates. The hot fumes of the whisky burned my nose. Sid was grinning. This kind of trouble was a charge to him. Right now he didn't need the extra thrust that whisky gave him.

The hell with it. I wasn't going to start it, either. That was the story of my life: forget every setback in a fifth of whisky. I pushed the bottle away and Sid laughed. The hell with him, too. I looked around restlessly.

There wasn't a cloud in the whole state.

I took the controls. Keeping us airborne was no job at all; we were birds with a full tank of fuel. But I needed even this little chore. I felt emotion surge through me like the white-hot burn of electricity.

I glanced again at the bottle of Echo Springs. I didn't want to start hitting that thing just because I was full of frustration and disappointment. I might out-drink Sid unless I kept busy. But suddenly all the old rages broke loose and began to boil—the rage against Judy and her Johnny, against Greenie, and Clark, and every blasted hurt I'd absorbed in the past fifteen years. It was a wild green bile of rage and I could feel it bubbling up inside me, thick and nasty.

The sky was still playing hell with our plans. No thunderheads showed anywhere and the sun kept on climbing hot and undisturbed. But I was dark and overcast inside, disgusted with myself for failing the simple task of starting that plane we needed so desperately and just as disgusted with that toy for failing me. I felt cold fury against Coates who was hitting the bottle now as if he wanted to pass out before we even found another plane. I hated the small town airports that we cased in the next two hours because people were moving around on them and they were too near to Bay City anyhow. Word might go out from that airport if those boys woke up and got to thinking about what happened—or what hadn't happened. Anyhow, it wasn't our fault we hadn't stolen that plane.

"What do we do now, pappy?" Coates said. His words slurred slightly, just enough to raise the boiling point in me.

"We find a plane." I said it coldly, clipping it, because I didn't want to talk to him. I was caught up in my own rage and it had to burn itself out, or I'd start to drink and I wouldn't stop until I had forgotten the whole mess.

"What's sweating you?"

There were too many angles bothering me to even discuss. "That plane back there," I said. "I ought to have gotten that thing."

He snickered. Where he was, there were no worries, or if you did have any, they were pickled. "We'll get a plane. Only you better choose a spot soon. Every field we see now is alive with people."

"All right." I yelled it at him. "I'm doing the best I can. You just keep nursing that bottle and let me alone."

I located an accumulation of black-tinged clouds to the east and headed toward them. The wind rose slightly and the world darkened as though I was suddenly looking through colored glasses, not stormy yet, but darkening. I had to hope for something. I felt better when we could sense the tickling of turbulence, and my disposition improved when single, large raindrops began to splat against our windshield.

"It's about time," I yelled at whoever is in charge of the weather up there.

Infinity seemed to close in on us, darkening; the rain increased, battering us in a fine brisk way. I could no longer see anything below us but moving treetops. We flew seventy miles in this overcast. Below us I saw the Spring Haven city airport, Greta Field. This was slightly larger than the field at Bay City, but the rain had chased even the pigeons. Puddles stood black in the runways and the close-clipped fields. The wind sock dripped dispiritedly.

I glanced at my watch. It was almost nine A.M. We had been in the air a long time. We were off-schedule. The time of the robbery itself had to remain flexible. We would move in on the bank when we hit Fort Dale, but I had hoped to exchange this first plane for a second at another airfield. At the rate we were moving, the Fort Dale bank would close before we ever got there.

I flew over Greta Field once, checking it out. The rain had dampened all the ardor in the afternoon pilots. The field looked wet and deserted. I knew better, there would be knots of men grumbling about the rain in all the hangars, in all the offices and the coffee shop. But our luck wasn't going to improve and this had to be good enough. I nosed the Cessna in for a landing.

"This is it this time, Coates. We don't make a score this time, we'll kill for today. Time is running out and we're not going to find a better deal than this."

"You'll make it, baby." He sounded confident, but I knew where his confidence came from. From the corner of my eye I saw him sucking at the fifth.

"Another slip like that one in Bay City—"

"You nuts? We've had our bad luck for today. It's raining ain't it? What more you want?"

I pinpointed the Cessna to a spot beside a bright green Aeronca parked beside a Greta Field runway. I looked the Aeronca over, glanced toward the distant hangars, nodded at Coates.

He took over control of the Cessna, sat idling it, watching me. I swung out to the cement and struck it running. I crouched low and raced across the runway and slid into the Aeronca. I set the controls, did all those things I ought to do, and said a swift prayer. I didn't expect much from this; they wouldn't even know where it was coming from. But the way it is, sometimes a prayer is all you need. The Aeronca sputtered into life, caught and purred with contentment as if it had been sitting here all this time waiting for me.

I turned my head, waved at Coates and moved the Aeronca out on the runway. It did not even cough. I headed into the wind, hearing the rain slap against the fuselage. I revved it hard, setting it for the quick run and then moved out, listening to the sweet purring of the engine, the whine of the wind lifting me.

I was airborne in seconds. I glanced back toward the ground being jerked out from under me like a wet, dirty carpet. There was no sign of any life on that field.

71

I checked on Coates across my shoulder. He was bringing the Cessna up on my tail. He was a shaky flier and the Cessna didn't truly behave for him, but probably with all that whisky in him, he believed he was smoother than the gulls.

I didn't have time to worry about that. Time was becoming a precious element in this business. I gave up any hope of trading the Aeronca. I liked the feel of it, the way it responded. The tension grew in me. I thought ahead to Fort Dale and the overcast skies and the bank and beyond all that I was thinking about Judy, and the money I needed so desperately, and the way the money would make all the difference for Buz Johnson. This was my last chance on this earth for any happiness.

I flew westward again and into clearing skies, but they no longer troubled me. I could see what I really wanted out there in front of me. I could see the jackpot.

Chapter Thirteen

I circled the abandoned strip near Berry Town without wasting too much time for a close check. Time that had been in our favor could turn like a tide and run against us. We'd cased this deserted strip. It was in an isolated section and we couldn't fool around any longer. I was still cobbed about being unable to start that plane in Bay City. Not even the way I had put this baby in the air from Greta Field really made me feel any better. It would have been so much smarter if we could have abandoned that first stolen plane in Spring Haven in exchange for this Aeronca. That would have covered our trail, and it was the way I had carefully planned it.

I signaled Sid I was putting down on the black asphalt strip. He waved, but I ignored him. He had been belting that bottle so hard that likely the whole field seemed overrun with little green men.

From the corner of my eye I saw something move near the weed-grown rim of the abandoned strip. There was a rain ditch over there that had been chewed out originally for irrigation or to make this field usable in wet weather. The work had been done a long time ago. Grass and fern covered the sides of the ditch, concealing the yellow scars of the bulldozer, and elder and small bay trees grew close to the edge, bending over the rain-swollen stream of water. I didn't bother about the ditch. The movement must have been made by a small animal. Sometimes the least movement like that will grab your eye when the earth is rushing up at you.

Too late I saw that the black strip was potted even worse than I'd allowed for. I had put down planes in bombed-out fields, but it wasn't any trickier than this was going to be. I eased back, kissing the ground, seeing a million chugholes in one glance, all of them brimmed with rainwater. They might be inches deep, a foot deep, bottomless. I leveled it, cutting to as short a run as possible. The whole plane quivered with the beating it was taking.

I shivered to match the plane. All we had to do was wreck the landing gear, blow a tire or break a shock, and we'd had it. We didn't have time to fly away somebody else's plane and I wasn't about to fly near Fort Dale in that Cessna, either.

The plane shook itself to a halt. I cut the engine and sat there a moment. Then I remembered something that pulled me taut. If this field had been a landing problem for me, then Sid was sure to wreck the Cessna. He couldn't make a decent landing on a dry field when he was cold sober.

I slapped the door open and jumped out of the Aeronca.

I stood on the ground with my legs spread apart, bracing myself for the instant one of his wheels hit a chug-hole and bowled him tail-over. The weeds came up around my knees, wet and thick. The broken runway wore rain cracks like pockmarks. I whispered at Sid under my breath, wanting to close my eyes as he brought the plane down, shakily, the wings dipping first to one side and then the other.

The man who first said that God protects fools and drunks was a perceptive cuss. Sid brought the Cessna down, wings wobbling, the whole plane seeming to hang back in protest, fear showing in the very way one wing quivered, tipping, and then the other.

His wheels touched the black asphalt, bounced, slipped

and water sprayed out both sides from beneath the tires. He touched again and the plane tilted to the starboard, then settled too squarely on both wheels, the tail going down too hurriedly. He rolled it along toward me, still gunning it too much, seemingly unaware of the million potholes gaping at him with wet eyes.

I breathed for the first time since I jumped out of the Aeronca.

Then, just before he taxied within thirty feet of where I stood, Sid suddenly wheeled the Cessna off the runway and went tail-dragging through the weeds toward a stand of trees opposite the rain ditch.

I yelled and ran after him.

He taxied in under some oaks at the rim of the field and was sitting there, grinning smugly, when I panted up to him. Oak limbs scraped the cabin roof, dripping along the fuselage.

"What the hell are you doing?" I managed to say.

His white eyebrows wriggled up and down. "We better hide this baby, Buz. No use taking a chance on it being spotted from the air while we're gone."

"You damned fool," I yelled at him. "You damned drunk. Get that plane out of there. We don't want to hide it. Man, the minute you hide, some hick wants to know why. Now get that thing back out on the runway."

He didn't like it but he pulled around, limbs scraping and whining against the fabric, and pulled back to the runway leaving his tracks in the mud and weeds.

I walked back more slowly, not liking any of it, wanting to get out of here. I had to watch Sid closely to keep him from thinking for himself.

By the time I'd walked back to the runway, Sid was out of the plane pointing at something at the rain ditch across the field.

I saw the two kids then. Their movement had snagged at my attention as I landed. They were fishing with cane poles in the irrigation ditch. They had stopped fishing when we came in for a landing and were standing at the crest of the embankment now, staring at us.

I glanced around, looking for a house to which they might belong. I saw nothing. Beyond the irrigation ditch was a hammock and past that I could see the turned land of strawberry fields. I could see no house, and hear nothing but silence. Sid and I stood beside the planes and the kids remained motionless against the elder and sweet bay growing over the ditch.

Suddenly Sid ran at them, yelling and waving his arms. I stood there, unable to move. He looked like some wild man or a scarecrow come to life. When he got near enough for the kids to realize that he was cursing and threatening them, and near enough they could see that frantic face and those wild eyebrows, they screamed in terror. They jumped across the ditch and ran off into the hammock.

Sid walked back, laughing and talking to himself.

I went to the Cessna and hauled out our suitcases. I stared at the fifth of Echo Springs. It was empty. I stood there with the bottle in my hand.

Sid walked over to me. He chortled and took the bottle. "I'm cutting down," he said. "Usually by this time of day I've had two of these."

Before I could say anything he hurled the bottle away from him and smashed it on the asphalt runway.

"My old friend the bottle," he said. "That's the way I treat all my old friends."

For a moment I was so full of rage I could hardly speak. I wanted to yell at him, but when I spoke, my voice was a hoarse whisper.

"You better pull yourself together, Coates. We got to land on this strip again. We got to take off. All we need is one flat tire."

He laughed some more, walking around kicking the shards and hunks of glass off the asphalt into the weeds.

He came back to the Aeronca, chuckling.

"You happy now?" he said. "Let's go."

I opened my suitcase, took out the coveralls and stepped into them. He watched me, his strange eyes owlish. Then he opened his suitcase. He stayed hunkered over it while time ticked on.

"Let's get a move on," I said.

"We got plenty of time. Let me have a drink."

He was struggling with the top of his second fifth. He giggled. "Man, the way you put that Aeronca in the air

75

back there at Greta Field. One thing, it don't make me feel bad I can't fly as well as you. Few men can."

"Get your coveralls on. Let's get out of here. We can't waste time now."

He was stumbling around trying to step into his coveralls. "Why not?" he said. He'd lost all sense of time. "They may not miss this Aeronca over at Greta all day. The way it was storming over there, who'd be going out in a plane?" He giggled again.

I stood there and gazed at the sky, feeling the nerves in my stomach tighten up again. We had flown out of the storm and into the sun. It wasn't bright, but there were no rough winds in this part of the state.

There were no rough winds in the Fort Dale area, either.

The noon sun glinted feebly on the steel towers and high tension wires strung across the stubbled field we had chosen just west of the little cattle town.

I cruised in low, circling the Aeronca from the south over the high-piled sand hills of the fertilizer plant that was across a narrow hammock from the field. The plant was a metal building, floury white in the sunlight, with tall stacks politely belching noon-hour smoke.

The hammock was an oak and pine grove and I sliced it thin crossing toward the field.

"Look at the hicks down there in that plant yard," Sid said. "Act like they never saw a plane before. Out there rubber-necking."

"Damn them," I said, keeping my eyes on the field.

"I'll lay you money they dash over to see why we land."

"You should have thought of that when you chose this field."

"Hell. Did I know we'd get here at noon?"

"To hell with it. That's no sweat. Sunday pilots land all the time in open fields to take a leak."

He pulled lovingly at his bottle. He giggled. "I'll run at them. They'll think I'm from Mars."

"Aren't you?"

He giggled again, bracing himself at the impact that loomed below us. This field had been plowed, harrowed and then left fallow for almost a year. It was rough. I forgot about Sid, concentrating on kissing just the tops of those weeds and moving across them.

It was shaky but when I pulled it up, Sid exhaled with pleasure. "Man, what you are is a genius."

I killed the engine, checked everything. The tension began to increase. From now on, flying had nothing to do with it. Robbery was new and alien to me, and no matter how carefully we had rehearsed, much of it had to be played by ear.

To my left there was a thickly grown woods of oak, black jack and pine. I saw no movement out there, no sign of any buildings. The road along the right of the field was a narrow country road that led to the fertilizer factory and the cattle land beyond. Across the field and through a grove of trees, I could see the red roof of the farmhouse. Nearer there was a ditch, a rusted wire fence strung between rotting pinewood posts. The hedgerow was thick along the fence with sumac and myrtle, blackberry briars and fennel, the sort of place where rabbits and birds nested. The noon silence crowded in when the sound of the motor died.

I put the pawnshop gun in my coverall pocket, stuffed some of the cloth bags in other pockets along with the silk stocking. Sid examined his gun and I could read pure delight in his distended eyes. He pushed it into his pocket along with his stocking and the rest of the cloth bags.

"This is got to be it," he said, talking to himself. "Now, I'm going to show 'em. I'm going to show them sons of bitches. They didn't want me at home, they didn't want me at school. First thing I ever remember is, nobody wanted me around. I was too much trouble. Well, by God, I'm going to be trouble now. I'm going to show them sons of bitches."

"You ready?" I said.

"Son, I was born ready for this."

We put on our dark glasses. I checked my wrist watch. It was twelve-ten. We had our plans for the robbery all set. We had allowed for the hike into town, the time it would require to hobble the local law, get into the bank and out of it.

"Let's go," I said.

We walked across the plowed field, climbed the

weed-grown fence. I stepped toward the road, then turned back and kicked the rusted wire down until it sagged and broke, leaving a place we could cross hurriedly.

"Man, what you are is a genius. Man, with you with me, I'll show those bastards."

Sid kept laughing and talking to himself as we walked north along the road. It was less than a quarter of a mile to the main drag of Fort Dale and another four blocks to the center of the town—and the bank.

A filling station/beer tavern stood on the corner. It was a square frame building with tin tobacco and cigarette ads nailed on its walls. The front ramps were shell-paved. A couple of paint-faded fuel tanks stood out front along with a battered water can and an air hose. A man in his fifties came out the front screen door and flies went up from it in a covey. A bread ad was tacked across one of the screen doors and seven generations of dust clogged the screens.

He ran out to the ramp beside his gas pumps, staring at us. He wore a denim shirt and levis. He needed a shave and would have felt better if he were thirty pounds lighter. His belt sagged under the pressure of his stomach.

He looked us over carefully. Strangers in the backwoods attract a lot of attention. He was a friendly man and so curious that his nose twitched like a rabbit's.

"Howdy," he said, grinning.

Sid glared at him. "Why?" he said.

The man went on smiling, but the effort pulled his mouth out of shape. We did not stop walking. He was not rebuffed.

"You fellows walk far?"

"No."

"Got car trouble, fellows? Leave your car back down the road there?"

Sid stopped walking and glared at the man until the poor guy got an uncomfortable sag in his flushed cheeks.

"For God's sake, Pop, why don't you go back in that little outhouse of yours and draw yourself a cold beer?"

His mouth drooped. "Just trying to help, mister. I can see you fellows are strangers."

"So go back to sleep."

He stood there watching us as we walked the next two

blocks. When we crossed the railroad tracks, I glanced back. He was still there.

We walked east, passed a feed store, a couple of cafes, a dress shop. I could not help staring at the red-brick building that housed the bank on the corner across the street. Sid was rubbing his hands together, smacking his lips.

Old men were sitting on boxes and benches tilted against the buildings in the shade. They eyed us as we passed. Some spoke politely and then leaned together, trying to figure what had brought us to town. Several cars were parked on both sides of the street, but business had quieted and there was a noon-hour lull about the village. A faint mist of rain kept everything damp, but there were still no rough winds, no signs of those thunderheads or that cold front that was due from the north. It was a great day for a picnic.

We went into a beer tavern across the street from the bank. Sid sat on a stool from which he could watch the bank front from the bar. He ordered a couple of beers. This was part of our plan, but I did not even sip at mine because I was tightening up and didn't know if I could keep it on my stomach. Besides, I no longer required any stimulants.

We did not remove our glasses, even though the tavern was dark and wearing them in the darkness struck the other patrons as silly. They glanced at each other, grinning about the screwball strangers who were already drunk.

We could not have asked them for a more satisfying opinion of us. I sat at the bar with my back to the door. The place was a narrow store that had been converted with a cheap bar, cheap tables and a few beer signs. I glanced over my shoulder, studying as much of the bank as I could. It opened on Main Street with two glass doors. Some construction work was in progress directly east of the doorway. On the west side of the bank was a drive-in window.

I checked my watch, nodded at Sid. We got up to leave and Sid hammed up his drunk. Anyhow, I hoped it was in part acting. The men in the tavern snickered and nudged each other.

We jaywalked across the street to the far curb with Sid walking in a wobbly manner that had everybody laughing at him. We looked at the stores and I chose the drugstore, half a block east of the bank. This was a very modern layout, brightly lighted, freshly painted and air-conditioned. The smell of chocolate syrup and cosmetics was strong. Two women clerks were on duty, one behind the soda bar and the other at the drug counter. When Sid stumbled across the entrance they regarded us with the kind of disapproval you'll only see in the faces of small town women who attend church regularly and have pledged to avoid whisky and the men who drink it.

He sat at the soda fountain. The girl behind it looked at us questioningly. She was in her early twenties, with lifeless brunette hair caught in a bun and net. Her mouth was tightly set. Sid semaphored her with his white brows.

"You sell beer, girlie?"

"I'm afraid you'll have to go to the tavern across the street." She gave us the haughty treatment as if we were something she wouldn't even touch to toss in the garbage.

"I been to the tavern across the street," Sid said.

"That's obvious."

I laughed at her self-righteous voice. She glanced at me. Her eyes narrowed slightly. "You seem more sober than your friend, mister. Or maybe I should say less drunk. You better take care of him. The police are rough on drunks in this town."

"Drunks?" Sid slapped at the marble bar with his open palms.

"That's right. We don't tolerate drunks in this town. You're liable to get arrested."

"Who'd arrest us?" Sid wanted to know. The other clerk and a couple of teenagers reading comics at the magazine rack were watching now, entranced. "You mean you got police in this town?"

She flushed. "We certainly have. You keep being so loud and you'll find out."

"Tough town, eh?" Sid slid off the stool and strode toward the pay phone on the front wall near the plate glass windows. "Don't look so tough to me."

He scrabbled through the fifteen-page phone directory. "What you doing, buddy?" I said, sounding alarmed.

"Looking for the number of the police station," Sid said, voice loud and daring.

"You don't have to look it up," the girl said in her

haughty way. "I can tell you the number. It's Twenty-six Blue."

He fumbled in his coverall pockets and found a dime. The two kids at the rack were giggling, nudging each other. The whole thing had a sense of unreality to me, too, but it was something that had to be done.

"You don't really have to call them," the girl said, still daring him. "That's the office, upstairs there, right across the street."

Sid stared through the plate glass window. I glanced up there, too. Through the opened window I could see a stout middle-aged man sitting tilted back in a swivel chair, his feet against a roll-top desk.

"Twenty-six Blue," Sid said "What a lovely number. I think I'll name my first child that."

"You better stop fooling around," the girl warned him.

"She's right," I said, laying it on thick and moving around at the counter as though worried and helpless.

The other people in the drugstore stood unmoving and watched open-mouthed as Sid punched in a dime and dialed Twenty-six Blue. We could almost hear the phone ringing in the upstairs office across the street.

We saw the stout man swing his feet off the desk and sit forward, picking up the receiver.

Sid said, "Let me talk to the police chief." Then he said, "Home at lunch? What's to happen to crime while he's home at lunch? . . . Who are you? . . . Constable Bill Gill? Bill Gill. You're kidding me. Nobody is named Bill Gill. . . . Well, you better get off your fat chunks and get over to the drugstore. We got a couple of out-of-town men over here. Acting drunk and mighty disorderly."

He replaced the receiver. None of the people in the drugstore spoke. None of them moved. The young girl was holding a magazine opened in her hands. She had forgotten it. We stood there watching the man in the upstairs window across the street. He replaced the receiver, sat a moment scratching his head. Finally he stood up, wearing a khaki shirt and khaki trousers. He put on a five-gallon Stetson hat and walked slowly out of the office.

A moment later we saw him come out of the stairwell onto the sidewalk across the street.

The counter girl spoke to Sid, voice self-righteous. "You're going to get it now. He'll take you to jail.

The constable was wearing high boots. He started to jay-walk across the street, changed his mind. He still hadn't decided if someone were joking with him or not. He got into a police car, started it, backed out of the angle-parking space. A plume of white exhaust billowed out in the faintly misting rain.

Constable Gill made a U-turn in the middle of the street and parked in the loading zone before the drugstore. Sid put his arm around my shoulders. "Come on, friend, let's go see the constable."

We staggered out of the drugstore and waited for him at the curb.

Chapter Fourteen

The constable sat behind the wheel of his car and stared at us.

He didn't suspect it, but our plan was ticking off just about as we'd planned. Sid's staggering around the streets of a small town might sound as off-beam as Sid himself, but except that Sid had had more to drink than I thought he would—more than most men could drink and still navigate at all—we were coming in strong and clear.

Making a scene in the drugstore and calling the cops might sound as if we were from left field. But we had talked it out, and the natural, vital first move was to block the local law enforcement out of action. Next, we had to have the use of a car. We hoped to accomplish both objectives when we met Constable Gill in front of the drugstore.

The female drug clerks and the teenagers followed us to the doorway and a few hicks gathered along the walk when the constable got out of his car. Gill watched Sid's antics for a few moments and grinned in a good-natured way as if he were enjoying a monkey in a zoo.

Constable Gill was a man of medium height, with pot-gut and weather-lined face. "Looks like you fellows have had too much to drink," he said amiably.

Sid was loud, pugnacious. "Yeah? Where would we get too much to drink in this hick town? There ain't too much to drink in this whole town."

The constable said, "Well, maybe you brought it with you. But one thing sure. You've had too much."

Sid spoke to me. "Come on, buddy. No sense yakking with this guy."

The crowd closed in, grinning. The constable was enjoying himself. Days can be long and dull in a village. "Where you think you're going?"

"What makes you think it concerns you?" Sid said loudly, so loudly the other sounds in the noon-hour seemed lost.

"I'm the law around here, fellow."

"You the law? You don't look like so much to me.

Somebody in the crowd spoke up. "Don't let him talk to you like this, Bill. Why don't you lock that smart guy up. Show him. He can't come in here like this."

"Yeah?" Sid's eyebrows wiggled. He shoved his face close to the constable's. "Why don't you do that? Why don't you try to do that?"

"Why don't you guys just behave yourselves?" The constable by nature was just a good joe. He looked uncomfortable. He would arrest us, but he was giving us every chance first. "I don't want to lock you boys up—unless I have to."

Sid yelled at him. "You not only don't have to—you couldn't do it!"

The constable exhaled unhappily. He caught Sid's arm and yanked him off-balance, giving him a shove toward the police car. "Get in that car. We won't have any trouble."

He stared at me, waiting. But I wasn't giving anybody any trouble. I went meekly ahead of him. Sid stumbled getting into the car, and I had no idea how much of this was pretense. I followed him, weaving slightly to make it look good.

I couldn't keep my eyes off that bank.

The constable went around the car, got in under the wheel, sucking in his gut a little to make it. He turned the ignition key, started the engine. His voice was cheerful, friendly. "Just don't give me any trouble, boys," he said, "and I'll let you sleep it off in the jug. Then you can go on your way."

"Why, that sounds good to me," I said.

"Sure. No sense in fines, anything like that. I know how it is a man likes to tie one on once in a while. Eh?"

"Yeah. That's it, all right."

The constable laughed and reversed the car from the curb. He pulled half across the street, making a long backward turn and heading east though the town building and jail was less than a block from where we were.

"Your friend has really got a load on," the constable said to me, making friendly conversation. "He could get you in a lot of trouble."

"Yeah. I guess you're right," I said.

Sid was sitting between us. He straightened suddenly and in a movement that I didn't even follow, he jabbed his pawnshop gun so hard into the constable's kidney that the stout man gasped out loud.

He slowed the car involuntarily and stared down at Sid's gun as though he'd never seen one before.

"What is this?" he said. "What is this?"

"This just ain't what you think," Sid told him. "Now you think hard on one thing—just how you're going to keep yourself from getting hurt."

"I'm starting no trouble." The constable said this with a little chuckle as if he still half-believed Sid was drunk and kidding. He was half right. Sid was drunk. But he wasn't kidding.

"Don't stop for that traffic signal," Sid told him. "Turn right and keep going until I tell you to turn."

Sid reached across the lawman's paunch and removed his gun from its holster. He shoved it in his pocket. "I'll just take care of that," he said.

"What you fellows want?"

"Just keep driving, Slob," Sid said. He cursed the constable for half a block without repeating himself.

The stout man was tense and starkly white before Sid stopped talking. Sid said, "You just better get it out of your mind that we're drunk, Slob. You do what we tell you, you won't get hurt."

"If I just knew what you fellows wanted—"

"You don't have to know, Slob. Just keep your mouth shut and keep driving."

We reached the outskirts of town. Sid chose a side road

and ordered the constable to turn the car into it. He slowed and made the turn, looking around helplessly.

Once he said, on a note of dim hope, "This can be pretty serious, boys. You can get in a lot of trouble. You give me back my gun and get out of the car. I'll still forget the whole thing."

Sid cursed him again until the constable was too numb to speak.

"Get it through your head," Sid yelled at him. "This ain't no game, Slob."

We didn't speak any more until we reached a secluded spot beside the cypress-black river that wound along the edge of the narrow road. This ancient side road looked as if it were the only change made in this changeless place. Huge oaks grew close against the pavement, great boughs arching low over the road so that they formed a dark tunnel through the trees and beside the water. Though we had come less than a mile from the center of Fort Dale we seemed to have entered a jungle, far removed from civilization. There were no houses along this lane, not even any fences, but only the trees and the sluggish river. Sid's muttering went on and on in the surrounding silence. His mounting frenzy was almost sexual. He had started a flow of words and he couldn't stop talking.

"Stop here, Slob," Sid said.

The constable brought the car to a halt. He killed the engine. Then he sat there with both hands on the steering wheel. His face was rigid. His eyes were wide, fixed on something he saw through the windshield.

"Get out, Slob."

The constable moved. He opened the door and got out. He moved as if he were very tired.

Sid slid across the seat, following him. He kept the gun lined on the small of his back. I got out the other side. We left both doors open.

Sid spoke across his shoulder to me. "What time is it?"

I looked at my watch. I had been checking it every two minutes since we got in the constable's car. "It's twenty of one."

"My God," the constable said. "What do you guys want?"

He glanced about as if trying to find some way of escape. The river looked black and deep and made a rustling sound against its banks. Under the oaks, a layer of old leaves covered the white sand. The branches above us were so thick you could see the sky only in patches through them. Bay, water oaks and elder grew tangled on the brink of the river and across it the brush was impenetrable.

"What you guys going to do?" The constable shook his head. "My God. I got to get home to lunch. My old woman is going to be sore. Hell. She gets sore when she has to wait lunch."

"Shut up," Sid told him.

"Mister, I'm just trying to figure what you got against me. Hell, I ain't even the sheriff. I'm just a constable here in town. I got a couple of kids. I tell you, you made a mistake. My oldest girl. Just started high school."

"For God's sake, shut your mouth."

"I'm just trying to tell you. You're all wrong. My wife. She'll be sore. The kids are home from school. You know—lunch hour. I mean—if you fellows—I mean, you got drunk. You're all mixed up."

"Slob. I told you. Shut up, shut up." Sid jerked his gun up, putting it within inches of the man's face. When he fired it, both the constable and I reacted. The sound roared in the silence, raced across the flat land and finally died away.

The constable staggered back from the concussion of the firing, the flashing burn of gunpowder. He clapped both hands across his eyes, momentarily blinded. He moaned, walking around, agonized.

Sid caught him and with a backhanded motion slapped the gun across the side of his head, catching him just above the ear, knocking his hat off and toppling him against the front fender of the car.

The constable crouched there, still unable to see, a jagged line of blood along the side of his head. The first thing he did when he could finally move at all was to pick up his hat and replace it on his head. He did not know what he was doing.

"Slob." Sid stood over him. His face was white and he was yelling. "You believe we mean business now, Slob?"

"I think so." The constable barely spoke aloud. Sid yelled at him, making him repeat it.

"All right," Sid said. "This is kind of just the start, Slob. From now on, you do what we tell you. You got that?" He brought the gun up and the constable cried out, throwing his arms up over his head. He cowered against the fender. This time Sid didn't hit him. He just laughed at him.

The constable lowered his guard at the sound of Sid's laughter and Sid hit him so hard with the side of the gun that the lawman staggered in a little half-running dance the length of the car. Then his knees buckled and he sank to the ground, his hands washing at his bloody face.

He pushed himself up on his elbow. His face was streaked with his blood. He shook his head. His voice trembled. "You didn't have to do that."

Sid strode to him and stood over him with the gun poised. "Don't tell me what I have to do, Slob." He wiped his hand across his mouth. "Now you know I mean business. In about five minutes you're driving us back to town. You got that? You're going to do just what we tell you—because I'd just love to put a bullet in your spine, Slob. You believe that, Hick?"

The constable nodded.

"All right," I said. "It's about time we started back." Sid prodded the constable with his shoe. "Get on your feet, Constable Slob. Don't be a fool. Don't be a hero. Don't try anything."

The constable nodded, pulling himself to his knees, still half-expecting Sid to hit him again. He dragged himself to his feet, braced against the car. He did not take his gaze from the gun in Sid's hand.

"Get in the car, Slob."

The constable nodded and got under the wheel again. He gripped it with both hands as if it were the last solid thing left in his life. The blood was running stickily down his face and along the corner of his left eye. He did not wipe it away. He did not seem to know he was bleeding.

We got in with Sid next to the constable, gun thrust into the soft flesh at the side of his belly, gouging.

"Drive back into town," Sid said. "Drive slow and drive

to the bank. We want to get there at two minutes of one. You don't get us there on the button, I'm going to gun whip your face, but good. You believe that?"

The constable nodded. He kept his face straight forward.

"You believe it good. Now let's go."

We reached the highway much quicker than we had gotten to the oak grove beside the river. Everything seemed accelerated. We whirled along as if we had been caught in a wind tunnel. We raced pell-mell. . . . I looked at the speedometer. We were moving at fifteen miles per hour.

It seemed like ninety.

Constable Gill pulled the car out on the highway. The first automobile we saw was a state highway patrol car. We all recognized it at the same instant. The constable caught his breath. I felt my heart pounding harder. I heard Sid's steady cursing, a wild crazy sound in the car.

"Watch yourself, Hero," he told Gill.

The constable seemed to understand the same truth that had occurred to me. Even if we shot him now, we could not hope to escape the patrolman. The constable didn't have to tell me what he was thinking: his wife waiting lunch, his two kids home from school. But his face was bloody. He was badly hurt.

Suddenly Gill swerved the town police car directly into the path of the oncoming state car.

Sid gasped and I sat there waiting. I saw another man riding with the state patrolman. The state cop glanced up, startled. Then he recognized Gill, grinned and waved. He pulled around us and kept going.

Sid cursed the constable for half a minute. "You know what was going to happen to you? I was going to pull this trigger if that jerk had stopped, Stupid."

Tears spilled from the constable's eyes. He nodded. He had known that. He had thought it all out in the space of those seconds.

Sid thrust the gun snout so hard into him the constable gasped involuntarily. "Don't be a hero. I warned you."

The traffic signal at the main street intersection was green. Several cars came toward us on the highway.

Gill speeded up, making the left turn directly in the path of the oncoming car. The driver's head jerked up. We saw him slam on the brakes so hard his car wavered. He pulled aside courteously.

Gill made an animal sound of frustration in his throat. He stepped on the gas.

Sid laughed. "Just keep it up, man. Fight me. When we do stop—I got it for you. I got it for you bad. I got it waiting." He laughed as if he could not conceal the pleasure he expected.

Gill kept his face straight ahead.

"Pull in at the west side of the bank," Sid told him.

"My God," Gill said. "My God."

"Name dropper." Sid laughed at him. "What's the matter? Is it your money?" He jabbed him with the gun. "Don't pull all the way to the drive-in window. Stop just past the walk. Don't make me hit you while the car's moving. We're going to have more fun when you stop."

It was 12:58 by my watch when the constable parked at the west side of the bank. There was only slightly more activity on Main Street than we had found when we arrived.

"You're a good boy," I told Gill. "You made it, on the nose."

"He's a good little slob," Sid said. "A real good little slob."

He reached over, cut the engine, kept the keys. Gill moved slightly toward his door and Sid jerked around, slashing the gun across his face. The lawman moaned and sagged against the seat.

"That's for free," Sid told him. "That's so you won't get any ideas."

Chapter Fifteen

The tension and excitement had Sid strung up tightly. He could no longer sit still. I couldn't dislodge the notion that Sid was getting the kind of charge from this you'd expect a man to get from an exciting woman—or perhaps the kind of sensation he no longer got from women. One thing I knew: Sid had desired this mission for more than the money he would collect. His greatest reward was

coming to him right now, and this made him more danger-
ous to me than any other obstacle I might encounter. Drunk
and incensed like a man in passion, he just couldn't be
trusted.

Sid nudged me and I thrust my hand in my pocket seeking the silk stocking. I closed my fist, pulling it out.

Sid was already working his stocking down over his face,
bumping the dark glasses away at the last possible second.
He worked it all the way down, sat there fidgeting, waiting
for me.

I couldn't escape the sense that everything was happening at an accelerated pace, going fast the way old-fashioned
movies gallop when run through modern projectors at 40
frames per second. Each breath took a long, labored time,
and we seemed to be moving in slow motion even while we
ran so swiftly that there wasn't time to think.

I fitted the stocking under my chin and closed my hand
on the gun in my pocket. I opened the door and got out of
the car. There was no one on the side street. There was no
teller at the drive-in window. I heard Sid shoving the constable out of the car ahead of him and after a fleeting eternity they came around the hood and joined me beside the
bank wall.

An awful stillness had settled over the town. I could not
help glancing upward at the darkening but cloudless sky.

"Go ahead, Slob." Sid pressed his gun against the stout
constable's spine. You could almost read the constable's
thoughts; he knew what a bullet would do to his spine. He
looked as though his knees were going to buckle.

I kept my hand in my pocket, holding the automatic
ready but out of sight.

We came around the side of the bank to the wide front
walk on Main. One man in overalls stood before it, a bank-
book in his hands. He had just come out through the glass
doors. He glanced at Sid and me, the stockings smashing
our features out of recognizable shape, and then he looked
at the constable and laughed.

"What is this, Bill—a Hallowe'en trick?"

Nobody ever thought about robbery in that back country.

But in that moment, the rube saw the blood smeared
across Gill's face. He had not seen the blood at first because

90

nothing prepared him for it. Now he saw it, and slow as he was, he began to react. Something was wrong. This was no prank. The blood on the constable's face was real.

Sid jerked his head at the hick in overalls. I moved over to his side and spoke as low as I could, "Back inside, mister."

"What is this?" Fear showed in the man's face. His mouth went slack.

"Do what they tell you, John," Gill said, and his agony throbbed in his voice. A decent, kindly man, he wanted to keep anybody else from being hurt unnecessarily.

For his pains he got the side of the gun against the back of his head. He stumbled forward ahead of us and thrust the glass doors apart, half-sprawling into the bank lobby.

Everybody in the bank stopped whatever he was doing and stared at the constable. That gave us all the time we needed. Seconds ticked away while Gill tried to regain his balance.

I forced the John character through the door ahead of me. The bank was practically square with double front entrance, the drive-in window at the west rear and a barred rear door beyond it. The tellers' posts ranged along the front west wall behind a high counter with wickets on top of it. At the rear of the room was a large vault and at the right behind a railing were the desks of the bank officers. Most of the desks were vacant at this hour. I saw two women tellers on duty, and a young man at a desk in the officers' quarters. I pushed John ahead of me to the first teller.

Just as Constable Gill caught his balance, supporting himself against the writing desk in the center of the lobby, Sid brought his gun down across Gill's neck and the big man slumped to his knees, clinging to the desk. Then his fingers slipped free and he slid face-down on the terrazzo floors. I heard the women tellers gasp. The young executive jumped up from his desk and ran through the railing gate, shouting, "Here now! What's going on here?"

Sid waited for him, legs braced apart near the desk. He called him some dirty names, enough so that the young banker began to understand and stopped running. Sid's voice quavered. In that swift-moving moment, I saw him trembling with tension and excitement, wound up and ready to burst. All I could think now was to fill those cloth bags and get out of there before he killed somebody. Robbery was one thing. Murder was another. I had not even considered it until I realized how much pent-up hate Sid had stored in him.

"This is a stick-up," Sid yelled at the banker. "You people do what you're told and maybe nobody gets hurt."

I motioned the two bank customers to move to the far wall and stand facing it, with their hands high against it, palms flat.

I tossed the cloth sacks at the tellers. Sid tossed his bags at them, too.

He pressed the snout of the gun against Gill's bloodied ear. "You dames start shoveling money into these bags or I'll blow this slob's brains out."

The tellers may not have assessed his threat at full value, but I knew better. I motioned with my gun, signaling them to hurry.

Constable Gill writhed on the floor. Sid caught him by the belt and helped him to his feet, cursing loudly. Gill wobbled unsteadily. Sid kept his fist caught in the man's belt, moving him around in front of him.

The tellers didn't move fast enough for Sid. He slapped the gun against Gill's bleeding head again. "Faster. You people hurry."

The tellers stared at the young banker. He did not hesitate. He nodded. "Do what he says," he told them.

"That's the way to jump when I speak," Sid said. He laughed, a fluting sound.

The young banker moved slowly forward in the lobby. The women worked swiftly filling the cloth sacks. As fast as they filled them, they shoved them through the wickets and let them fall on the floor outside. The bags plopped against the terrazzo with a plump, full-bellied sound. I moved forward and gathered up each sack.

I could hear Sid's wild laughter behind me.

The young executive must have decided Sid wasn't watching him. He lunged toward Sid, going off both feet in a standing tackle. Sid's laughter rocked against the ceiling. He whipped the butt of his gun down and the crunching sound it made against the banker's skull was the loudest noise in the town.

The young banker struck the terrazzo flooring on his face. For some seconds he did not move.

"You stinking hicks seem to think I'm kidding." Sid shook the fat man by the belt. The constable staggered and almost fell. He was almost unconscious. "Fool around with me, and find out."

The man on the floor stirred, tried to crawl away from Sid. He was lying now with his head near the doorway.

I gathered in the fourth bag, watching the banker. I wanted to yell at him that he needed only to keep trying to be a hero to make Sid kill him. Beyond him through the glass doors, I saw a farmer standing motionless on the walk. He was peering inside the bank, face blank.

The banker raised his head, speaking to the man beyond the glass doors.

"We—we're being robbed."

The farmer did not move. He stood there staring at the man on the floor. I saw Sid watching them and knew he was going to shoot the banker. I yelled at the man on the floor: "Shut up. Haven't you sense enough to keep your mouth shut?"

The banker turned slightly, blinking up at Sid's gun. For the first time he appeared to realize how nearly dead he was.

He slumped back to the floor and Sid laughed. For a moment the banker stared at the expressionless face of the farmer through the glass doors. At last he spoke, his voice dead: "Go on. Get away from here."

The farmer did not move.

"We got to get out of here," I told Sid.

I had collected all the tight-stuffed bags now. My arms were loaded with them. All the money I had dreamed about all these weeks. All the things I wanted. And all I had to do now was get Sid out of here before the whole caper came unglued.

I backed away from the tellers' counter, going toward the door, back-pedaling, watching the women.

"Let's get out of here," I told Sid again. "Let's scram before our luck runs out."

I glanced at a wall clock. We had now been inside the bank for seven minutes.

I was at the door. But Sid did not move. He did not want to relinquish his sweet hot excitement and sense of power. He stood there waving that gun, working himself up to a climax of painful pleasure that he would never experience again. It seemed as if he could not leave until it ran its course. He cursed the women tellers, warned them not to move.

He released Gill's belt. He shoved and the lawman sprawled forward, slipping on the floor. He struck his head against the tellers' counter and sagged to his knees. He stayed there with his arms covering his head. Maybe he expected to die and did not want to hear the sound of the gun.

"Come on." I pushed at the glass doors. "You got to put on a show for them?"

Sid laughed, a wild, distorted sound. He backed across the foyer to the doors. One of the women moved and he screamed at her. She gasped and froze where she was.

Sid glanced down at the banker on the floor at his feet. The man tried to crawl out of his reach.

"You people stay where you are."

He jerked up the gun and fired across the top of the tellers' counter.

The women screamed and ducked down behind the counter. And then, abruptly, from the street, I heard the wail of a siren.

Somebody had called the sheriff.

I did not wait for anything else. I spoke once more to Sid. I ran out on the walk, carrying the bags pressed against my chest. Above the tops of angle-parked cars I could see a black police sedan like Gill's speeding on Main toward us from the highway intersection.

"There he comes," I yelled at Sid.

Sid stared at the speeding cruiser. He laughed. I ran past him and went around the corner. He followed, ran around Gill's car and got in behind the wheel.

He was ripping off the stocking mask as he ran.

I landed on the car seat, slammed the door behind me. Sid thrust the key into the ignition, turned it. The engine whined into life. I sat there hugging the bags of money.

Sid whipped the car around on the side street, bumping over the far curb.

94

The sheriff's car was almost at the bank when we turned right and speeded west toward the railroad.

The police car slowed at the bank. People ran out yelling at the sheriff. We got a break because evidently the sheriff thought Gill was driving his car.

But the sheriff's car didn't pause in front of the bank for more than a few seconds. I glanced back. It was speeding after us.

"Rich man!" Sid raged at me. "You hate being a rich man now, you bastard?"

We rumbled across the railroad tracks, the car shimmying crazily. It skidded sideways almost across the street before Sid could straighten it out.

"He's right back there, Sid."

"Hell with him."

"Sid!"

"What's wrong, rich man?"

"There's the beer tavern. Slow down. That's the turn. You can't make it."

"My God. I didn't know it was this close."

Sid stood up on the brakes, twisting the steering wheel at the same time. The car seemed to tilt on two wheels. Rubber screeched, burning long black streaks across the pavement.

The tavern door slapped open and Old Nosey ran out to the gas ramp and stood there staring at us.

We missed the turn by a good six feet. The car skidded into the mud and clay at the edge of the pavement. I felt the front wheels sink into the ooze.

Sid shoved the gears into reverse. The car screamed in protest a moment and then lunged backward from the mud. Sid shifted into forward drive and stomped the accelerator in one movement.

"My God," he yelled. "My God. I need a drink."

I glanced over my shoulder at the sheriff's car. For the second time, we got a break in time. We raced into the side road and I watched the other car.

Sid whooped and yelled with glee. He jerked his head toward the beer tavern. "I oughta take a shot at Old Nosey."

"You keep driving. The cop back there couldn't slow down enough to make the turn, either."

"Man. We're rich. That's why."

I could see our plane parked in the vacant field to our right. Sid stepped on the brakes. The car skidded off the narrow macadam and rolled a few feet into the ditch. Sid didn't even bother cutting the ignition. We scrambled out of the car before it stopped. I saw the break in the fence I had stomped down. Using both arms to hug our money, I ran through the break and across the weeds.

The field was rough when I tried to run through it. Every weed and every abandoned furrow seemed to have been put there to delay me.

Sid was behind me. He had his gun drawn. I did not slow down. The sheriff's siren whined down to a whimper as he skidded to a stop behind Constable Gill's car. Another car stopped behind the sheriff's.

When the sheriff and the men in the second car moved to get out, Sid snapped off two quick shots at them. One shot smashed into the windshield of the sheriff's cruiser. The next sang across the hood of the other car, and the men in them paused.

Sid's crazy laughter and his shooting made those men cautious. They crouched low to get out of the cars, careful now to keep the cars between them and Sid's gun.

Sid was loping toward the plane at an angle, half-turned to watch the road.

I scrambled into the plane, dumping the bags on the floor ahead of me. I slid into the seat, slapped at the ignition and felt the instant response of the plane motors.

With the sound of the engine, the whole mad crazy pace slowed for me. I was all right now. Even with the bags of money on the floor, I recognized a truth: I wasn't a robber, I was a pilot. We were going to succeed now. Once I was in a plane, nobody could stop me.

Sid ran toward me.

The cops had crouched low and dived into the hedgerow. Somebody fired through the fence. A bullet splatted into the Aeronca windshield. They had some idea of putting the plane out, stopping us before we could take off. Sid returned their fire and they ducked close to the ground. I got the plane in motion, the cabin door hanging open.

Sid fired one more time and lunged toward the plane

door. His hands caught, slipped, and I was moving past him.

He jerked his face up, staring at me. I heard another crack of gunfire. Another bullet slapped into the plane glass. I leaned over, reached out as far as I could and snagged at Sid's coveralls' collar.

He slid his gun into the cockpit, caught at the plane seat and I held on to him, gunning the motor, moving faster. I heard the men yelling from the hedgerow, the muffled crack of gunfire.

"Buz." Terror squeezed Sid's voice thin. I tightened my grip on him. I felt him using his arms to propel himself into the plane. His legs were dragging through the grass. And then suddenly his legs were free. He thrust upward, landing inside the plane on top of the cloth bags of money. He twisted around, caught the door and slammed it.

At that moment, after the shortest run of my career, I put the plane into the air. I did not even know if we were flying into the wind. I knew only one thing. I had to get aloft and I did, pulling that Aeronca off the ground by sheer frantic will.

Then there was only the wind around us and under us. The shouting of the Fort Dale men receded, and we could no longer hear the sound of their guns.

On my right I saw the steel strands of the high-power wires. We were close, too close. But I didn't really worry. I was moving and I was in the air.

Sid gasped noisily through his mouth. He lay with his head back, a man physically and emotionally exhausted. "My God, Buz, I didn't realize a man could handle a plane like this. Any man."

"Rich man," I said.

Oh, it felt good up there, all right. I was breathing, it seemed to me, for the first time since we had landed in Fort Dale.

Chapter Sixteen

The cars looked like toys below us down there beside that field. The men resembled ugly little animals, growing smaller every instant, crouched in the hedgerow and then running out into the field as if reaching for us. I looked back and could not see their guns any more. They could not touch me now.

The road was filling with cars that raced in from the town and from the fertilizer plant south across the oak and pine hammock. The cars sped to the field, parked on the shoulders, spilling men. They all ran out into the field and then stood there, impotently, staring up after us.

"Head out of here," Sid yelled. He reached behind him, opened his suitcase and got another fifth of whisky.

"You still need that stuff?"

"Man. I don't need it now. What I'm doing now is celebrating."

"You better wait until you got something to celebrate."

Sid took a long pull at the bottle. He shivered. "Celebrate or not, man, I had to have that." He offered me the bottle. I shook my head. "I'm all sucked out, whipped. I never felt like that before, Buz."

"Yeah. You were wild."

He nodded. "I had those people by the short hairs, Buz. You just don't know. I felt like God. I felt stronger than God. I could look at those bastards and decide if they went on living or not."

"My God."

He drank again. "That's the trouble with you, Buz. You didn't get your kicks from that job. That's because you haven't been pushed around like I have. Every new school they put me in, I was on probation. They didn't say so. They didn't have to. They had my record from the last school. They knew how many schools had fired me. I had to take it. They rubbed my face in it, and I had to take it, and then when I couldn't take it any more, they never asked why, or who started it, they fired me. And the whole dirty business started all over again. But nobody kicked me around today. Nobody. I told them to move. By hell they moved." He roared with laughter, and then laid his head back as if he were emotionally depleted.

He held the bottle up, gazing at it. He took another long drink. Then he reached behind him, lifted one of the suitcases forward, opened it across his knees. He untied one of the cloth bags and for a moment we stared at the tight packs of green, forgetting everything else. He emptied the bag into the suitcase and those fresh, crisp bills gleamed and caught all the light in the cabin.

He counted the money, loudly, rubbing it against his hands, washing his hands in it and pretending to use it to pat dry the perspiration rings under his arms. He rocked with laughter. He would not quiet down; perhaps he could not. He counted the money aloud, and finally, when he reached the upper thousands, I fell under the spell of it, I began to be hypnotized by that much tax-free money.

He stacked it tightly and neatly in the suitcase, still counting.

As he emptied each bag, he turned it inside out and then tossed it from the plane. We would watch it waver and flutter and then disappear behind us. When I checked the sky, I saw no sign of thunderheads, but I tried not to think about this. We had come this far. Just a little bit more and we had it made. We were rich men. I tried to think about the things I wanted, the things I was sick with wanting.

"Seventy-eight five." I listened to the chant of Sid's voice. His counting mixed with his laughter. It seemed to me the act of robbery was the end of it for Sid. He might spend the money, but standing in that bank, threatening those people, actually holding their lives in his hand, scaring the wits out of them, ordering them around, yelling and cursing and getting away with a robbery—this was what Sid really wanted, what he had been looking forward to all the time. The money was gravy. Perhaps he had never even really dreamed ahead to the possession of all this money.

"I think I'll take about three weeks in Bermuda," Sid yelled. "While I make up my mind where to go on my vacation."

"Vacation?"

"Man. We've worked hard. We must have worked hard. Look at this loot. We're rich. And all my life my sainted father has told me that you never get rich unless you work hard. Little man, we've had a busy day. We've worked hard. And now we have earned a nice, long rest."

He spilled out the last bag of greenbacks, rubbing the flat of his palms against the hard, tight packs.

"What you plan to do, Buz?"

I was looking forward to the difference this money was going to make between Judy and me, the way it would make it possible to go to South America as an equal with Greenie. My whole life was going to be different.

I shrugged. "Who knows?" I said. "Hell, I'm too rich to plan anything."

He laughed. "That's the way to talk. Remember that fool stuff you talked about before we got this money? Marriage. Some kind of job in South America. I let you talk then. But man, even you must see it's all different now. You can buy babes by the dozen. And work? What you want to work for? There's plenty more where this came from, ain't there?"

"You mean you'd go through this again?"

"Man, that's what I mean. This is living. Baby, this is habit-forming."

I studied the hazy sky. I shivered, thinking that I hadn't had a drink all day, simply because I was working at something that took all my powers of concentration. I had to have something I really wanted to do or this money wouldn't change a thing. I would drink myself into something like a wet bar rag.

"I still know what I want," I said "The only difference is, now I can buy what I want. Now I can live the way I want to live."

"That's what I said." Sid was caressing the stacks of money. "No use to get married and go to work. Not now. Now that you can live the way you want to."

I didn't answer him. He was blowing spit bubbles as he counted the last stack of money. His face pulled in and out of shape like overheated plastic. I could not keep my gaze off the sky, and I kept praying for that cold front with its rough winds.

I snapped on the radio. "I'll see what I can get on the weather."

"If you can't get the kind of weather to suit you, we'll buy you some weather. Just what you want." Sid giggled at this wonderful new idea.

The music came in on the standard band. It ceased abruptly. A cool-cat voice purred, "A news bulletin from Spring Haven. At noon today Ron Harver of River Grove

100

Estates reported the loss of his Aeronca, pocketed at Greta Airfield, Spring Haven. Aw, come on, fellows, bring back Ron's plane."

Sid laughed until he had to wipe away the tears.

"They're looking for an Aeronca—this one," I told him. "And they've been doing it for the last hour and forty minutes. Laugh about that."

"Man, I'm laughed out."

"The Coast Guard, the Forest Service and the police can put planes in the air. We've got to junk this thing."

I checked the mileage indicator. We seemed to be floating in a lazy way through the haze, getting nowhere, though I was pushing the Aeronca so hard that it had developed an engine knock. Now it seemed an infinite distance to that Berry Town strip where we'd parked the Cessna.

"You got it all in the suitcases?" I asked Sid.

"Ninety thousand bucks," he said, voice awed.

"Ninety thousand bucks." I felt the sweet saliva fill my mouth. I swallowed.

"You know what half that is?"

"It's a nice day's pay."

"Man, I can live a month on this. A month. I don't have to worry about money for a month."

The music ceased again. The announcer said, "Shortly before noon today, a daylight robbery cost the National Bank at Fort Dale almost a hundred thousand dollars in cash. The two robbers wore stocking masks and coveralls, and according to the Fort Dale police they escaped in an airplane. Within minutes, word of the strange air robbery and amazing getaway was radioed through out the state. All law enforcement agencies including the FBI are converging on Fort Dale."

Sid snickered. "Yeah, all you fellows. Run down to Fort Dale." He stopped cackling. "Hell, Buz, what's the FBI want in this for?"

"Something you should have looked up while you were casing that job. Robbing a bank, that's a federal offense."

"Well. What you know? Ain't that a lovely thought? All these years the government's been robbing me with compulsory taxes and now I'm hitting back at them."

I gestured downward, motioning him to shut up. The

announcer continued, "All airports in Florida have been alerted to watch for the two-place sportsman's plane. The make and the color were not learned immediately—"

"We got one break," I said. "We might still make it to Berry Town."

"You better hope they know what they're looking for before we get in that Cessna."

"—Planes from Air Force and Coast Guard bases have joined the air search. Forest service fire towers all over the state have been put on watch for the small plane."

"We got to junk this thing," I told Sid. "We got to get rid of it and fast."

The music cut in again. I felt as though I were alone in the plane. Sid sat there, sucking at that bottle. He kept one hand gripping the suitcase full of money.

"Get those coveralls off," I told him. "Put them in that other suitcase. Put everything in it—dark glasses, stockings, everything."

I worked out of my coveralls, wriggling them down over my body, stepping out of them. I shoved my glasses and the stocking in the pockets. I put the gun on the seat beside me.

"Think we might have to use these babies some more?" Sid's voice sounded odd. He patted his gun.

"Are you crazy? If we get over the bay again, we drop them."

"I don't buy that," Sid said. "We—might need 'em."

"That's right. And that's when we'd be fools to use them. It is just like telling everybody in the world that we knocked over that bank."

"Then what?"

"What are you talking about?"

"What do we do after we ditch the guns?"

Sid looked as though I'd asked him to parade naked down Main Street. In fact, he would have preferred that. I wanted to yell some sense into him, curse him for the fool he was. But I kept my voice low. "What's the matter with you? You got a big sexy charge out of what you did, huh? You been playing cowboy and Indians today? You want to shoot some more? Well, we're playing it just the way we planned. We flew down to Verona City. Remember? We flew back to Sunpark. We don't know anything else. That's all we know. We don't need guns to put that over."

"Man, I feel helpless already."

He sighed, and mooned over the gun I refused to let him use any more. He held it in his lap, fondled it, thinking. He took another drink. Then he tilted his head and gave me a wild grin. "All right, Buz. Anything you say. You're the boss, Buz."

We pushed our coveralls into the suitcase, locked it. Ahead was a forest of trees. I saw no sign of habitation. The spot looked good to me because it was cypress, standing brown-dead and moss hung. This meant a swampy, inaccessible area. They might find the stuff in there but it would be a long, wet search.

I flew in low and dropped the suitcase containing the clothing into the swampy undergrowth. I exhaled heavily and climbed for altitude, not even looking back.

The music stopped, the radio crackled a moment. "Word here is that a small two-place plane, a bright green Aeronca, has been spotted by a Forest Fire Service tower in the ridge section about fifty miles inland from Sunpark—"

"Now they know what they're looking for," I said.

"Yeah. That's us," Sid whispered. It was a sick sound, spewing across his lips.

"Well, we know what they know."

"God damn 'em. They're not going to take my money from me. Not now. Not after all this. Not after all we been through."

"—Three Coast Guard planes and an Air Force pursuit plane have been put into the air to overtake the green Aeronca which authorities believe was used to make a getaway after a bank robbery earlier today in Fort Dale—"

"Damn them. Damn them." Sid wasn't laughing now. He glared at the speed indicator. "My God, Buz, I could crawl faster than this."

"Watch for them," I told him. "If they get on our tails, we won't be able to touch down at Berry Town."

"That's crazy. You nuts? We got to get out of this crate."

"Sure. But what's the sense of changing planes if they're watching us?"

"Buz—"

"Yeah?"

"Isn't that Berry Town? Up there?"

I nodded, unable to speak. "Watch for planes, Sid," I said after a moment. The relief flooded through me, as if cooling a high fever. "I'm putting this baby to earth and under those trees."

I clipped treetops coming into that abandoned strip. I was traveling too fast and that asphalt runway was potted, but I could not slow down. I felt as though the devil were riding my tail.

We touched, jumped, and bumped and skidded off the runway. I wheeled it hard around and rolled through the grass toward the trees with motor roaring.

Sid's face was white. Jolting across the field made him bounce like a monkey on a string. "Man," he said. "Man. I wish you'd take it easy. This kind of flying makes me nervous."

I taxied the plane in under the wet trees, cut the engine. I took one quick check. We were leaving nothing in the plane. I didn't worry about fingerprints because I knew they had to be clearly marked on a flat surface to be worth anything to the police. But it didn't matter if we forgot anything or not. When they located the green Aeronca here, they would know it was the robbery plane because the windshield was pocked with bullet holes. All I hoped was that we got away quickly enough so no one ever linked the Cessna with this plane, this field.

Sid was hugging the suitcase against him. We carried our guns in our fists. I scanned the field. It appeared deserted. There was no sign of the two kids. I warned Sid about using that gun, but by now I no longer trusted him at all. If anybody frightened him, or crossed him, or appeared suddenly from the underbrush, he would shoot at them.

He opened the door, got ready to leap to the ground.

"Wait a minute," I said.

"What's the matter now?"

I glanced at the Cessna, like safety waiting for us on the runway. I didn't want to spoil it. I wanted just what Sid wanted, to race across these weeds, get in that baby and get out of here. But we had to be more cautious than ever from this moment forward.

"It might take a couple minutes longer," I said. "But there is something we better do."

Sid's face was working, mouth slack, now taut.

"Yeah?"

"You walk ahead of me. But slow. I'll hang on to your belt. Every time you lift your foot, I'll put mine in its place. If we leave them just one set of footprints in this mud, that ought to give 'em fits."

Chapter Seventeen

I put the Cessna in the air, pushing it hard, gunning it, and we headed south by west.

I was flying scared, fighting a tightness in my chest. I knew what it would do to our plans if we were caught northeast of Sunpark. Sure, we might get away with the lie that Coates was piling up flying time, but nobody was going to believe he could fly in his condition. On the other hand, once we got southwest of Sunpark, I could make almost any story stick. I kept watching for the pursuit planes. I did not see them, but I didn't have to see them. I knew they were there.

"Can I relax now?" Sid said.

"You better," I said. "We can get ourselves snarled up from here on unless we keep it in our minds that we haven't been out of this Cessna—and we haven't been north of Sunpark."

The music was abruptly tuned out on the radio again. An announcer said, "The descriptions of the two daring daylight robbers in the Fort Dale National Bank holdup have been broadcast—"

"What?" Sid yelled at the radio, leaning toward it as though he were going to smash it with the gun butt.

I jerked my head at him, motioning him to keep quiet. He stayed bent forward, listening, his pale brows knotted.

"Constable William Gill of Fort Dale was taken to the Fort Dale hospital with serious cuts and bruises about the head after severe gun-whipping at the hands of one of the

105

bandits, but he feels that he can give accurate descriptions of the fugitive pair. 'At least one of them,' Gill is reported as saying, 'The tall one. I would know his voice anywhere if I hear it again.' Gill repeated that he would never forget that voice."

"Oh, fine," I said. "You really sang them the arias, too."

Sid did not speak. His face was a mass of ruts and grooves.

"The taller man is reported to be about six feet tall, very slender with thin, sallow face, sandy brows and hair. His hair appears to have been bleached. 'He looked middle twenties,' Gill said. 'He moves with a gangling gait and has long, thin hands, very white and uncalloused.'"

"He might as well have given them a photo," I said.

"I could have autographed it for him. The son of a bitch. I should have hit him harder."

"—The other robber, according to Constable Gill, is five or six years older than his partner. He has black hair and a dark complexion. He spoke very little and Gill would not be as certain of his voice. Both bandits wore sunglasses until they donned stocking masks for the actual robbery. Gill said these masks were pulled on just outside the National Bank at Fort Dale. He said the second thief is about five feet six or seven inches tall, stocky, with a wide mouth and a straight nose."

"He doesn't pin you down so good," Sid said.

"Don't feel good about it. Those descriptions are going all over the state right now. They'll go to Sunpark. They're close enough."

"So what do we do? Keep flying? Out of the state? How about Cuba?"

"No. We can't outrun that pursuit plane. The first thing to do is ditch these guns and then stick to our story about Verona City. We can make it if you keep your head."

"Buz, I'm telling you. You're a fool."

We were out over the Gulf now. I wanted to skirt Sunpark as widely as possible. I pushed back the window and tossed out my gun without thinking twice about it.

"Let it go, Sid."

"Buz—"

"Sid, I know you're a fool. But not that big. They'll have

the slug from the bank wall. There may be a slug in one of those cars they chased us in. You let 'em have that gun and they'll pin you down at Fort Dale. With that constable to listen to your voice in a police line-up, you're dead. Now get smart. Toss it."

He let it go, but it was a difficult thing for him to do. He clung to it until the last second and then watched it strike the water in a silver splash.

I couldn't say why but I felt better when those guns were gone. Guns weren't going to buy us anything from here on in.

I wheeled the Cessna south by east and we flew across a chain of uninhabited islands between Sun Bay and the Gulf. The sun shown now, weakly, but we had not yet seen any other planes. This might have been an unexpected break we got because the weather was better than forecast and other sports planes must be aloft today. The pursuit jobs might be wasting time chasing down false leads. I hoped so.

I found a small, deserted island with a wide, white stretch of beach and put the Cessna down.

"The tide is coming in," I warned Sid. "So we don't have much time. We don't have any time to waste. We got a lot to do. Let's hit the beach."

We jumped out with Sid carrying the suitcase. I found a clump of cabbage palmettoes about ten paces through sea oats from the beach. I motioned to Sid and we stashed away the suitcase. Sure as hell, the police were going to find the Aeronca. All these weeks, I had figured maybe Sid and I would not even be suspected. If there had been a storm as the weather reports predicted, the Aeronca might not have been missed all day. But we couldn't count on any of that now. We would just have to let the money cool out here for a few days.

Sid was gathering loose palm trunks and palm fronds, sea oats, cabbage palmettoes. As soon as I had marked the place where I stashed the loot, I helped him. We piled a small mound of weeds, fronds and tree trunks out on the beach, above the reach of the tide, but far enough in the clearing that we could recognize our mark from the air.

We worked as swiftly as we could and all the time Sid was complaining about stomach cramps.

"You drank too much."

"The hell I did. I'm scared."

"Why are you scared now?"

"I been scared. Ever since we threw away those guns."

"My God, Sid, you been watching too much TV."

"Can I help it? They have them in every bar I visit."

We checked our mound of debris to be sure it was weighted down securely enough so the wind couldn't rip it apart. We ran across the beach then. Far out on the Gulf I could see a small boat. Clouds were banking up on the horizon, but not near enough to mean rain.

Sea gulls whipped down to stare at us curiously. The tide was coming in fast. It licked at the tires of the Cessna as we got in. We had to take off before that water softened the hard-packed beach; the white sand above it was too treacherous. We had to stay out of it.

I started the plane, revved it and we sat there a moment making a last check on everything. I tuned in the radio. Then I tested the wind with my hand out the window and headed into it.

We skidded away and up over the water. The gulls couldn't have done it smoother. Both of us looked back at that mound of weeds we'd piled on the beach.

The first report we got on the radio was bad. Sunpark County police had located the Aeronca hidden under trees at an abandoned airstrip outside Berry Town. The windshield of the small plane was potted with bullet holes. The robbers had vanished, leaving nothing but footprints leading away from the Aeronca. The deputy sheriff had ordered bloodhounds brought to the airstrip and meantime plaster casts were being made of the footprints. Clear specimens were imprinted in the soggy mud. The prints seemed to have been made by one man which momentarily puzzled the police.

"Bastards," Sid said. "They don't waste much time."

I was thinking of something else and it made me as ill as Sid claimed to be. I was remembering those kids that Sid had chased away from the Berry Town landing strip. When they came forward to tell the county police about the plane that had put down there and the one that had followed, they would have a description of the Cessna. They could not fail. What kid doesn't instantly recognize every make of plane?

We flew along the coast, keeping it in sight. The wind rose and we hit airpockets that shook us badly.

I put down at the Verona City airport.

"What if they question us?" Sid said.

"About what?"

"I don't know. They might have the description of the Cessna by now."

I glanced at him. His face was drawn and his eyes were fixed on nothingness. Not even the whisky could lift him up any more. He had gotten clued in, too. Those Berry Town kids would remember the two planes.

"It can't be helped," I said. "We got to find your friend as an alibi that we were here in Verona City."

"Hell, we were supposed to be here this morning."

"Engine trouble. We can make that stick. There are two of us."

I taxied up close to the Verona City hangar and we got out. This airstrip was a one-hangar and control tower deal with inadequate runways and a few sports planes parked in a line. A couple of men in the hangar doorway spoke to us but they didn't seem excited about anything. Sid asked if they had a public telephone and one of the men pointed to a booth inside the hangar.

I watched Sid lope across the cement to the booth.

"Not much of a day for flying," one of the men said to me.

I decided to nail our alibi down hard. "We hit some rough pockets, all right. But we've had trouble all day. Engine trouble. Took us all morning to get down here from Sunpark."

"Oh? You fellows from Sunpark?"

My stomach muscles tightened up. But then I saw he was not suspicious, merely being polite, making conversation. I glanced toward Sid. He was inside the booth.

I felt sweat. Still, it would be good to have these men witness that we were in Verona City and had had engine trouble to delay us.

The phone rang inside the hangar office. One of the men said something and went to answer it. There was a roaring in my ears and I heard nothing clearly. The other man stood there watching the Cessna, the sky, nothing.

The man inside the office lifted the phone, pressed the receiver against his ear. For some moments he listened without speaking. I knew something was wrong, something that concerned Coates and me. I don't know how I was so certain. I tried to tell myself it was conscience. If this man hadn't received any word on us in all this time, what would he be hearing at this moment? He didn't glance toward me. Then I saw he had straightened and was staring through the doorway at the field control tower.

Feeling sick, I turned and looked at it. It was nothing more than a tinted-windowed booth on steel supports out across the runways. A man inside the shadowed windows was standing up, talking on a telephone and pointing at something down on the field. This was too much coincidence for me.

I heeled around and looked at Sid. He was still in the phone booth. The man inside the office was nodding.

I walked as casually as I could make it on rubbery legs toward the phone booth. I wanted to yell at Sid. He did not notice. I got all the way inside to the booth. I wanted to look over my shoulder. I needed to know what the two men at the office were doing. But I knew I'd better keep it cool.

"Sid."

I kept my voice level. He turned, and when he saw my face he read the danger signals loud and clear. He replaced the receiver without even saying goodbye. He stepped out of the booth, frowning at me, puzzled.

"Let's get out of here," I said.

He nodded. We walked out of the hangar and across the runway at an angle going to the plane and yet not returning near the office. I glanced toward it. The man at the phone had called his buddy inside and he was standing just within the office door. The man at the phone was poking around in his desk drawer, searching for something.

"Faster," Sid said.

I nodded. In order to keep abreast of him, I looked as if I were running. I felt the sweat cold along my ribs.

"One thing sure," I said. "Somewhere the law has gotten a description of the Cessna."

The two men came out of the office, walked toward us from the shadows of the hangar.

"Don't look at them," I told Sid. "No matter what happens. Keep walking. Don't look at them."

Sid nodded. He shoved one hand in his jacket pocket and took longer strides.

"I think one of them has a gun."

"No matter what they've heard, they can't be sure. They won't shoot unless they're sure."

He swung up into the plane and I slid in under the controls. I switched on the engine and it kicked over.

I heard the men yelling something.

They hesitated a moment; then they ran toward us.

"Get out of here," Sid said.

I gunned it. The radio phones sputtered. The tower was repeating a request for us to identify ourselves. I didn't even bother answering.

I took one quick gander at the wind sock and moved out on the chute. The two men were standing on the runway. They yelled and waved at us. One of them had a gun all right. He shook it in his fist but he didn't use it.

"It's all over, Buz."

"The hell it is."

"No, Buz. Why kid ourselves? They got a description of the Cessna. We can't even go home now."

"We got to go home. That's for sure. Hell, have we got guns? Have we got money? What about your friend in Verona City?"

"He wasn't home. Hasn't been home all day."

I felt Sid get the shakes. He looked as if he were going to be sick. I yelled at him, warning him to hang onto himself.

I was in bad shape, but one of us had to think. At first the news about his friend sounded pretty bad. It put us on a spot. But then, when you flipped the coin, and looked at the other side, it was better. "Wasn't home?" I said. "Fine. Then he can't say we didn't get here this morning. We were late, sure, but we ran into engine trouble. We went up again and put in some flying time. We came back. It's going to work."

"Stop being an ass, Johnson. It ain't going to work. They

got our descriptions. The Aeronca. The Cessna. Me. You. We can't even put down at any airport. We're up here in the air and we're stuck here until they catch us and force us down."

"It's got to work," I yelled at him. "I didn't go into this thing to have it flop. They haven't got us yet. And for God's sake, don't buy the idea that Clark owns the only silver Cessna in the state. Nobody has anything on us. Keep your head and we'll be all right."

"No. It's no use, Buz. We could run—for Cuba. That's all."

"That would get us an Air Force pursuit plane on our tails and that's all it would buy."

"Then we got to ditch this crate somewhere, separate and hide out. That's all we can do. We hide out until it quiets down, try to get the money and run."

"Why don't you just take an ad in newspapers telling them just how guilty you are?"

"You got a better idea?"

"Yeah. Act like you got some guts. Suppose we have to face a few questions. We got answers."

"No. It's no use, Buz. I won't have them hounding at me. That's the story of my life. I won't go through it."

"You've got to."

"No. I couldn't make it. Hell, it was all I could do to walk across the ramp back there knowing those two men were going to stop us."

"But we made it."

"Yeah. We made it that time. Now we're up here where the whole damn country can spot us."

"Nothing is easy," I told him. "What's the matter? Nothing but a gun in your hand makes you a big man?"

"It helps."

"You can make it worse on us by going chicken, Sid."

"I'm not chicken, Buz. It's just that I can't face jail. Buz, that's what my whole life has been. A jail."

"Now what are you talking about?"

"I'm finished. I'm through with the whole caper."

"Now I know you're nuts."

"No, Buz. I want out."

"Are you flipped? We got almost a hundred grand back there on that island."

He was silent a moment, rubbing the palm of one hand across the back of the other. He stared out of the plane, head averted from me.

"Take it, Buz. You take it. You can have it all."

My insides chilled. "What are you planning?"

"Nothing, Buz. I want you to put the plane down on a lonely road somewhere. In a field. I don't care." He was searching the sky, turning his head like a radar screen. "You let me out, Buz. You can have all the dough."

"Oh, boy. And you were a big shot in that bank with a handful of gun."

"I can't help it, Buz. I'm all right. As long as I can fight. As long as there's a chance to save my neck. It was like that in the bank. I could pull it off because—"

"Because you had a gun."

"All right, Buz. Say what you want. But it happened back there when you made me throw that gun in the Gulf. I knew then we were finished."

"You'd have been finished if you kept it on you."

"No. That's where you're wrong. That's where we're different. I got to have something that makes me stronger than other guys. I haven't got it now. They can kick me around and I'd have to take it. And I can't face anybody like that, Buz. Not any more. I can't be arrested. I'm telling you. You let me out. You swear I wasn't with you today. I got airsick—I am airsick—you had to put me down somewhere. Tell 'em anything. I wasn't even with you, today. I'll go to a motel somewhere. I'll hide out. That's the way it's got to be, Buz. I can't face anybody."

I glanced at him, slouched there with his head hanging down over his chest. His neck was long and scrawny. He looked old, a hundred years old, and finished. And slowly I got as ill as he looked, because I began to see that here was the boy I had trusted and he could blab us both into the chain gang, and the first time any pressure was applied to him, he would do it.

I grabbed his arm, shook him. "Snap out of it, Sid. If you keep your head, we can collect—"

"I don't want it, Buz. I told you. You can have it. All of it. Just swear I wasn't with you today. I won't say anything. I swear. I'll never say anything."

My voice got as cold as I felt. "Until you get drunk sometime? My God, you think I can ever trust you after this? Why didn't you tell me what you were, before we got into this thing?"

He sat there a long time, slumped inward, hands jammed into his sports jacket pockets, taking it, thinking it over. He did not attempt to defend himself. All he wanted was to get out of this plane, anywhere, alone. He was silent so long I thought he wasn't going to speak at all. When he did speak his voice was a husky whisper. "I didn't know, Buz. I didn't know it myself."

He turned and faced me, eyes agonized, mouth twisted.

"Buz."

"Yeah?"

"Don't let's have any trouble, Buz. Not you and me."

Something flared, hot and angry, in my head.

"You threatening me?"

"It doesn't have to be that way, Buz. I don't want any trouble with you. Put me down, anywhere at all. You got all the loot. I swear it."

I felt myself tightening up, all through my body. Coates had spoken in a whine, but I sensed an implied threat behind every word. I tried to see into his face and couldn't do it.

"You afraid I'll talk, Buz? I won't."

I was as cold as something chopped out of marble.

"What's the gimmick, Sid?"

"Buz. Put me down. I don't care where we are. You hear me? I just want a chance to run, to hide. Before a plane gets us spotted. You put me down—we have no trouble—it's quits. I know nothing."

My hands tightened on the Cessna controls, sweating. I no longer believed anything he said. If they caught him, he would talk all right. He would never stop talking. If I let him out, he would hide until he got thirsty, and then would hit the taverns. If I went back without him, I'd have to frame a hundred new lies, and the more lies you tell, the easier they break you down.

I measured him carefully. I could stop his babbling by killing him. But I felt something quiver at the nape of my neck. I had the feeling this was what he was waiting for, a chance to strike at me. I shook my head. I had never thought the idea of killing would occur to me this side of a war. Killing in a war was bad enough; I never could square that killing with my conscience no matter how many medals they pinned on me. Finally, in the night, I'd tell myself it was a matter of killing or being killed myself, and then I could sleep for a while.

Sid watched me, hands thrust in his jacket, waiting.

Chapter Eighteen

"Please, Buz. Touch down in that cow pasture. Half a minute, I'm out of here. You got it made."

I didn't answer him. I was thinking how it had to be. If Sid got away from me, he would drink, and when he drank, he would babble and never stop babbling until we were in the pen.

The sky was darkening. This bugged me. Oh, fine, I thought, clamping my teeth together. Now it's going to rain. Now we'll get that rough weather.

"You're sticking with me, Sid."

"I can't, Buz. I would. I can't."

"You are. Whether you want to or not. We're going back. I'll talk. You keep your mouth shut." I glanced toward a wrench beside my foot.

"It's what I'd like to do, Buz. But I'm thinking about both of us. I couldn't face anybody. I couldn't fake it off. You let me out and I'll scrounge in somewhere and hide out for a while."

"No," I said. "And, Sid. There's something on your mind."

"What you talking about?"

"You got some hot idea. But I warn you. I got a wrench beside me. You make a move—I'll use it on you."

"My God, Buz. My God. We're buddies. What kind of talk is that?"

115

"Just so you know. We're going to stay buddies. I don't want you to start anything that might spoil it."

It got silent in the cabin, a surly silence with a chill in it that had nothing to do with the rough winds we were flying into, or the rain beating against us.

Suddenly Sid yelled, "Buz!"

"What's the matter?" I was having my troubles. We hit an airpocket and the plane bounced like a yo-yo.

"Behind us, Buz. Two planes. They're headed for us as though they had us spotted."

I lifted the nose of the Cessna, climbing. I glanced over my shoulder and saw the planes. They were coming in at five o'clock, fast.

I climbed frantically toward the banks of thunderheads, forgetting Sid, and the wrench. Whatever he had on his mind, I didn't believe he'd try anything as long as we were running scared.

"They really got us," Sid yelled. "You get the picture yet, Buz? They've spotted us. They're going to keep us flying until the gas runs out—and then they got us. Damn you. You begin to get clued in yet?"

I swore at him. "The hell with that. They haven't stopped me, and when they do, I know nothing, and you keep your mouth shut."

"Hell, Buz, what's wrong with you? They're reading us on a radar screen right now. Don't you know that? They're in contact with those pursuit planes and God only knows how many others."

I wasn't listening. The rain splatted against the windshield. Above us the thunderheads were miles deep and lightning flashes were ripping them open every few minutes. A real turbulence up there, and I was flying into it.

"Give up, Buz. For God's sake. Give it up." Sid took a drink from the whisky bottle and then stared at it, eyes distended because suddenly the whisky was no good and he could not escape in it.

"Shut up, Sid. I can lose 'em in those clouds."

"Buz, put it down or I'm taking over."

"Talk like that any more and I'll kill you." I lifted the wrench, hefting it.

"Don't talk like that Buz. Not even kidding."

"I'm not kidding."

He looked around helplessly. The only reason he didn't jump was that he didn't have guts enough for that, either.

"My God," he whispered to himself. "My God. My God."

His nose began to run. He sniffled and wiped at it with the back of his hand.

I pressed the Cessna to its limit and held it at top speed. We raced into the thunderheads and the lightning bolts were suddenly all around us, hot charges screaming past, cracking and spitting in our eyes.

I kept moving and finally Sid spoke in a low voice. The other planes must have turned back.

I glanced at my watch. It was almost four P.M. Just three hours ago we'd robbed that bank in Fort Dale. Three hours. A lot had happened. They had our descriptions, descriptions of the planes, fields alerted to keep us from landing, pursuit ships in the air, and the dissolution of our fine partnership. The only thing that kept that partnership from total extinction was the wrench beside my fist.

It had been a long three hours.

I figured we were less than ten minutes south of Sunpark. "I'm heading home," I told Sid.

He didn't answer. He seemed to have forgotten me.

"Keep your mouth shut, Sid. I'll talk."

"Sure, Buz. Anything."

"We got to stick together now. Probably Sunpark International is the only place they'll let us land."

"Anything."

We flew out of the center of the storm and the rain subsided.

"We'll be all right as long as we tell the same story. We flew to Verona City. Your friend was gone. You put in some flying time. We had engine trouble. We flew back to Verona City. He was still gone. We haven't even heard about the robbery."

"Yeah? Why didn't we stop when those guys yelled at Verona City?"

"Hell, how did we know what they wanted?"

"And why didn't we answer the control tower?"

"Who needs a jerk in a control tower? So we were drinking. That's going to cover plenty. Everybody knows we drink."

"It ain't going to work, Buz."

"The hell it's not. I'm on my way to a job in South America with a nice stake in my pocket. I don't mind telling a few lies to make that work. You just keep your face shut, and I'll get you out of it, too."

"You better, Buz. You better."

I glanced at him. "You're still threatening me, Sid. What gives?"

He shrugged. His face twisted and he didn't answer. That plane cabin seethed with hatred. I knew the one thing on his mind. How he could kill me and get away with it. And I—what had happened to me? First, I had let myself get involved in a robbery, and now I was measuring Sid, choosing a place to strike with that wrench when he jumped me.

What is it they say? It takes just one drop of poison.

Chapter Nineteen

I pushed the Cessna hard, running away from the thoughts that had infected me. If I ever got out of this, I never wanted to see Sid Coates again because it would always remind me of how I wanted to murder him. I shivered a little, wondering if the money was ever going to be any good to me.

I laughed. It was an odd sound in the plane. It sounded more like Sid Coates than me. I was going to get that money. I could forget what I went through to have it.

It was something I would have to learn to live with.

"Like a broken arm," I told myself aloud. "Like a broken arm that's suddenly all turned to solid gold."

Sid glanced at me, but did not speak.

I thought ahead to getting this plane back to Jimmy Clark and Hangar 2. Because of Judy I wanted to keep the Cessna out of the robbery. Still, they might have a reception waiting for me. But this was the last act, and I was going to make it. All I had to do was keep Sid quiet and put on a convincing exhibition. Then I could pick up the marbles and go home.

I flew into Sunpark International, contacted the control tower and requested permission to land. The airfield looked huge and busy, but I detected no signs of extraordinary activity. All the action appeared routine. But then the radio man hesitated and I felt my heart sink. When he spoke, his voice had an odd inflection. He was being too casual. I warned myself to hang on. They couldn't prove anything as long as Sid and I told straight stories. As scared as Sid was, he would keep his mouth shut.

They okayed a runway, gave me wind direction and velocity. I shoved in the stabilizer, moved the controls, putting the Cessna down, unconsciously searching the area around Hangar 2 for police cars. I couldn't see any.

I taxied to the hangar and there was Jimmy Clark's smiling face on that sign. It won't be long, I told smiling Jimmy Clark's smiling smile. I'll clear out of here, a rich man.

I killed the engine, motioned Sid to get out. He sat there for what seemed a long time as if paralyzed, unable to move.

I saw Jimmy Clark and a stout man in a cheap brown suit come out of his office and walk toward us. I glanced at Sid and we moved across the cement to meet them.

"Good God." This was the first thing Clark said.

"What's the matter with you?" I hoped my voice was level.

"Where you been? All day? You flew out of here before six A.M. Where you been?"

"You know where I been." I made it belligerent. I glanced at the stout man, wondering if Jimmy were trying to impress him.

"Now wait a moment," Jimmy said. "I don't know where you been. I don't know anything of the kind."

"The hell you don't. You know Sid Coates hired this plane for the day, for a flight down to Verona City."

"Oh?" There was an odd quality in the smile on Jimmy's face. "That where you been all day? Verona City?"

"That's right. Except for some engine trouble."

"Engine trouble? What kind?"

"Oh, just the gas line. But it gave us fits for a while."

The smile widened on Jimmy Clark's face. This grin was

genuine anyhow, a grimace of inner secret pleasure.

He glanced at Sid. "That where you been, Coates?"

Sid just looked at him.

"That's where we been." I admired my own voice. I said this as if it were the most natural and honest statement in the world.

"Quite a day," Clark said. "This is going to cost you plenty, Coates." Coates just stared at him. I said, "He's good for it. You know that."

"I don't know that."

I shrugged. "Well, that's between you and Coates."

"I don't know about that either," Clark said, pressing it hard, and glancing at the man in the brown suit. "You arranged to take the plane."

"I told you Coates wanted to hire it."

"Yes. That's what you said."

"What is this?"

Clark stopped smiling. He suddenly looked as right-eously indignant as a man retailing the hottest gossip. "I'll tell you what it is. There is a kind of mess, Johnson, and the way I see it, it's all your making."

"Why don't you break down and tell me what's the matter?"

The stout man smiled in almost a sheepish manner. "Why don't we just step into Mr. Clark's office and talk this over?"

Nobody had to tell me he was from the police. The size of his feet had nothing to do with it. There are two kinds of lawmen: the loud ones and the overly-polite. This boy belonged to the latter persuasion. He was still a cop. I glanced at Sid. Something was building up in him. I could almost see the shadows smoking and swirling around in his eyes. He kept cracking his knuckles, wrinkling up his face, sniffling. He didn't look at anybody.

The stout man touched my arm and I shook him off.

"Why don't you tell me what it's all about?"

"In the office," he said in that firm but humble way.

"Who are you?"

Clark came up with that phony smile again. "Why, I'm sorry I didn't introduce you, Johnson. This is Mr. Fred Baylor. Mr. Baylor is from the sheriff's office."

I glanced toward Sid. He was making little noises under his breath, writhing as though his suit was tightening up on him.

I kept my voice casual. "From the sheriff's office? What do you want with me?"

The man shrugged. "Nothing, maybe. Maybe it's something we can just talk out. Why don't we just go in Mr. Clark's office and try?"

"Sure," I said. "Why not?" I saw them glance at each other but I went on playing it straight. I was glad Sid had kept quiet. Now all that worried me was that he might be building up to some kind of explosion. All we had to do was keep remembering they had nothing on us. They couldn't prove anything.

I moved my head toward Sid and then walked ahead of them into the hangar and through the door to Clark's office. I slumped in one of the chairs. Sid sat in a straight chair near the far wall. He was chewing at a hangnail and still emitting those faint noises.

Clark went around his desk, sat in his swivel chair. He sat there fumbling with a cigarette lighter. Baylor leaned against the doorjamb in a very casual attitude, as if he just didn't care to sit down.

"Something has come up," Jimmy Clark said. "You see, Johnson, you've put me in a spot, kind of."

"It's kinda sticky, and that's the truth," the sheriff's man said. "You see, it so happens there are just two silver Cessnas like that one out there in the whole state of Florida. Would you believe that?"

"So? What's this got to do with Sid and me?"

"Nothing, I hope," Jimmy Clark said, and that was the phoniest sound he ever made. "You see, this other Cessna belongs to a man on the East Coast. They checked already and got sworn statements that his Cessna wasn't in the air at all today. They had quite a storm on the east coast."

"And this kind of puts you two fellows in a bad light," Baylor said. "You see, a silver Cessna was spotted in a couple places today. And it looks like it was used in a bank robbery."

"Bank robbery?" I got to my feet. "What kind of thing is this? What are you accusing me of?"

Baylor looked unhappy. "We're not accusing you, Mr. Johnson. Hell, the whole town knows the war record you got. All we want is for you to tell us where you were all day. That way, we can clear this thing up about Mr. Clark's plane and no embarrassment to nobody."

"I'm pretty anxious about that," Clark said. "I don't like the idea of anybody even thinking a plane of mine was used in a robbery."

"What kind of robbery?" I said.

The stout man scowled. "I told you. A bank. Where you been all day you haven't heard about it?"

I told you where I was, too. I flew down to Verona City. Coates wanted to see a friend down there."

"You know where we could get in touch with this friend down there?"

I glanced at Coates. He was rubbing his palm against the back of his other hand, wriggling in the chair. He did not lift his head.

"No. I don't. He wasn't there when we flew in in the morning. Then we flew around, and had engine trouble. It took a long time. We took a second run to Verona City. You can check that. Then we hit a storm coming back. Head winds. It got pretty rugged, slowed us down."

"You had more engine trouble on the way home?" Clark said.

"That's right."

And you and Coates flew down to Verona City this morning?" the deputy said.

I amended this to suit them. "Well, no, Sid wanted to get in a little flying time—"

"Where did you fly?"

"Out over the Gulf mostly. I don't know exactly. Sid wanted to get in some hours. Then we flew into Verona City and—"

"You told us that."

I shrugged. "That's all I can tell you. That's what I'll keep telling you."

"Your friend Coates seems to have hit the bottle," the deputy said.

I shrugged again. "Well, if that's all. I might as well get on home. I got a lot to do."

122

"Yeah," Sid said.

"Well, that's not quite all. You see, we'd like both of you to wait until we check what you've told us. Like I say we don't want to cause no embarrassment. And if the folks in Verona City substantiate your story—"

"Why wouldn't they?"

"Well, I don't know. I hope they will, Mr. Johnson. Like I say, we hate to have things like this happen. A man with a fine record like yours and all. But, well, the fact is, a Cessna answering to the description of Mr. Clark's was seen near Berry Town—"

"Berry Town? Are you nuts? That's north of here."

"And you didn't fly north of here?"

"No. Why should we? Verona City is the other way. I don't like this. You guys act as if you think I robbed somebody—"

"Yeah," Sid said.

There was movement outside the office. The deputy stepped aside, dragging off his hat, and Judy walked past him into the office. I had kept my gaze away from her photo on Jim's desk. Now here she was. I didn't want her to hear this, didn't want her to see me handled like this. I felt my face muscles sag. I felt the bleak emptiness spread inside me. She was wearing her stewardess uniform, neat and trim and young and clean. Why did she have to hear this?

She looked as if she had been crying.

"Buz," she said. Her voice quavered. I saw her glance at Sid and then look away, visibly trembling. It hit me that the first moment I was suspected, Jimmy must have run to her with the whole mess.

She stared at me as if trying to see inside me. I felt my face going white and bloodless. All my blood seemed to be congealing in the pit of my stomach.

"Buz—you—didn't do it?"

"Hell," I said. "You, too? You believe everything this joker tells you?" I jerked my head toward Clark.

She cracked up then and cried aloud. I said, "God, it's funny how everybody is willing to believe the worst about a guy.

She covered her face with her hands. I moved toward her but Clark came around the desk and brushed me aside.

"It's all right, Johnson," he said. "I'll handle this."

"Looks like you've already handled it."

He ignored that, led her to the leather couch. He sat down beside her, kept whispering to her. I turned my head, stared out at the sky ramps and the overcast skies.

That was when I saw the three police cruisers pull in before the door of the hangar, blocking it. Police piled out of the cars and walked toward the office. They didn't draw guns. Everything was still very friendly. Only that hangar opening was barred.

Judy stopped crying when two detectives entered the office. She sat there beside Clark, her face starkly white, withdrawn, watching them.

Baylor said, "Howdy, Captain. I been talking with Mr. Johnson and Coates here about this case. They seem to have a pretty fair alibi."

"That so?" The captain said. He was a beefy man who smelled of cheap cigars. He didn't seem too impressed. The look he gave Coates and me labeled us something pretty foul.

I winced, not because I cared about myself but because Judy saw it. I remembered giving myself the romantic smoke that I was Jesse James of the air, Robin Hood in a plane.

Seeing myself with the captain's eyes, I recognized myself for what I really was. A thief. Renegade. I was a failure and a guy who couldn't make it and had pulled a job he couldn't handle.

I glanced at the smile on Clark's face and I saw something that had escaped me until now. It tied me in knots. I could have gotten away from Baylor and Clark, and that was why they had stalled me. When I contacted the tower, they called the sheriff. Then Baylor and Clark got orders to stall us until he could send a squad to take over. And that's what they had done. I couldn't hate Baylor; this was his job. No matter what guff he gave me about feeling bad about this, it was still his job. But Clark I could hate. It was easy. He wanted me taken in, dragged down as far as possible, even if I were later proved innocent. It made him feel that much better than I was.

Baylor said, "Only thing, he says Coates was flying. But Coates looks pretty potted. Otherwise they sound clean."

"We'll get to Coates." The captain said it very quietly, but the room suddenly lighted up the way a pinball machine does when tilted.

Coates straightened up in his chair, keeping his hand in his jacket pocket.

I heard Clark laugh across the room. It was a savage sound. I didn't look at him. I could not force myself to touch Judy's gaze even for a second. I wanted her to think I was better than I was, not lower, even now when I had lost her.

"Why don't you take it easy?" My voice sounded hollow. "I told you people where Sid and I were. Check on it."

"Don't you worry about that," the captain said. "We'll check."

I heard Judy catch her breath. I was getting the full treatment. And she was witnessing it all, the way they stripped the flesh off me.

The captain said, "For my money, you and Coates never got to Verona City until this afternoon. We got word you and Coates flew in there and then ran when they tried to question you."

"I didn't see anyone trying to question us." I said.

"Oh, Buz." Judy's voice was a stricken whisper.

"So what if they did?" I said. "I didn't know they wanted us. And that sure as hell proves we were in Verona City."

The smile left the captain's face. "You were in Verona City well after two this afternoon. We take your word for that. But before that, you were on an abandoned airstrip outside Berry Town. We got a plaster cast of footprints made on that airstrip at Berry Town. We dropped by your apartment, Johnson—and Coates' place. We checked those prints. And I got the word for you—those casts match your shoes, Johnson."

In a way it was funny as hell. Who would have thought my feet were bigger than Coates?

Chapter Twenty

"If you two men will just come along with us," the captain said, "and don't make any trouble, it's going to be a lot easier for you."

I stood up. "The hell with you. I'm not the only guy in this country who wears that size shoe."

The captain sounded tired. "We got a lot more than that, Mr. Johnson. Believe me. But we just don't want any trouble with you two men."

"Well, you got it." My voice was loud. I was bluffing. Maybe they knew it. None of them moved. I glanced at Judy. She knew I was bluffing; it showed in her face. I jerked my gaze away. "You accuse me of something, try to arrest me—"

"Buz." Judy stood up, though Clark tried to hold her arm. Her voice was soft, but it stilled everything in that office. "Please, Buz, don't make any more trouble."

I didn't look at her. I knew my face was bloodless. I didn't know how long my knees were going to support me. "Don't tell me what to do. I haven't done anything and I'm not going with these guys just because your smiling stepfather stalled me around so they could frame me."

"I'm sorry about that, Buz," Clark said. "Truly sorry. It was my plane. I didn't want any trouble or notoriety. I had to go along with them."

But Judy was staring at him, her face puzzled. She shook her head, her voice odd. "No, Jim . . . No. Buz is right. About you. You wanted to go along with them. You told me—over a week ago you told me you were sure Coates was planning something crooked and was pulling Buz in on it. You told me you were sure they wanted to use your plane on some crooked business—yet, today—you let them take it." She shook her head again. "You wanted this to happen."

"Judy." Clark shook his head, the phony smile gone.

The captain said, "Stand up, Coates. Let's go.

Coates stared at him a moment, then stood up slowly. He towered above Judy, even slouched as he was, standing beside her.

The captain touched my arm. "Let's go, Buz."

"If you take us in, you better have some charges."

He looked pained. "Buz, do I tell you how to fly a plane? You're not the first guy ever had to go down to the station. Don't let it bug you. I tell you, we've sent for this Constable Gill from Fort Dale. He takes a look at you and Coates—he says you're not the guys—why, you're free as the air."

"That won't be good enough."

The way Coates spoke struck me like an electric charge. I jumped as if I had been burned. Everybody in the room turned to look at him.

He had caught Judy's left arm in his left hand and had twisted it behind her back. She was bent forward slightly, wincing with the pain. But this wasn't what stopped everybody in their tracks. He had a gun placed against the middle of her spine.

"Anybody moves," he said, "she gets it, right in the spine. You like to see that, Captain? If you want to see that, you just so much as clear your throat." And then he cursed him with some words he hadn't even used in Fort Dale.

For a moment I could only stare at that gun. It hit me in an instant, though I'd completely forgotten it until now. Sid had Constable Gill's police positive. I saw now why he had thrown his pawnshop gun away. He had never intended to be without a gun. And when I saw this, I began to see a lot of other things too, none of them pleasant.

All the police were standing in front of Sid. None of them would have moved anyway because we could all see his hand trembling on the police positive. The slightest sudden move and he'd press that trigger. Only one man in the room was in any position to strike at Coates with any hope of surprising him. This was Jim Clark. But he sat as if petrified on the leather couch. Jim did not even look up.

The cops stepped back when Sid thrust Judy before him. He jerked his head at me, motioning me through the door. I walked out. He ordered the other police away from the doorway and then he came through it, sweating, his eyes distended and wild, the gun thrust against Judy's spine.

The police kept their guns in their holsters. None of them was about to endanger Judy's life by trying to jump Coates.

"Go ahead, Buz." Coates voice was something new now; there was power in it, and I saw by what a thin line Judy's life hung.

I backed away watching him and the police, going toward the Cessna. Something had happened in my chest. I felt as though a stone had obstructed my breathing.

"A fool thing, Buz." The captain spoke after me, his voice

very low. "What a hell of a way to waste yourself—a man like you."

"Shut up!" Coates cursed him some more.

We moved out under Jim Clark's sign; past the police cars. When we reached the Cessna, Sid turned, raging with laughter, watching the cops. They had moved forward and taken positions against the cruiser. But he knew they were not going to fire. If they didn't hit Judy, his bullet would snap her spine.

"Get in, Buz."

"You damn fool. They can shoot us out of the air."

"Get in, Buz." He cursed me now, the way he had cursed the tellers in the bank. The partnership had been dissolved for some hours, only he had neglected to tell me.

"Now, God damn you, I've listened to you. I've tried it your way. Now we're going to do it my way. Or your doll gets it in the gut."

"Sure," I said. "You'd like that, wouldn't you? Your day won't be complete until you've killed somebody. It was going to be me, wasn't it, Sid? Only now, Judy will do as well."

"Get in the plane." He screamed it at me. He was shaking. I got in under the controls. He thrust Judy in ahead of him, on her knees on the floor. Laughing, he got in and sat, holding her arm twisted against the small of her back, the gun fixed on her.

"Put it in the air, Buz."

I switched on the engine, listened to it come to life. I taxied it away from the hangar. The police had drawn their guns. They ran out on the cement, but none fired.

Coates sat watching them, laughing.

"What you think you're going to do, Coates?"

"What I was planning to do all along, sucker. Only now I'm doing it sooner. Get this bucket in the air and fly south. The faster you fly, the more you do like I tell you, the longer your doll stays alive."

I glanced over my shoulder as I jerked the tail of the Cessna around. The prop wash made the police grab their hats. I gunned it, feeling it lift its tail and race along the sky chute. Two of the cruisers reversed from the hangar and sped along the runway after us. I felt the wheels come free and then I was climbing.

I was less than a hundred feet in the air when I let it side-slip. Coates yelled at me. He caught Judy's hair in his hands, shaking her head as though she were a doll. "You want her dead now? You want her dead now?"

I brought the plane up straight and kept it there climbing.

"God damn you," Sid yelled. "You make it stall, you son of a bitch, and I do kill her."

I glanced at Judy, huddled on the floor. She had not spoken, had not lifted her head to look at me. That was fine. Nobody had to tell me I had lost her forever. I had lost her a long time ago, only now the official score was in.

"Go ahead," I yelled at Sid. I laughed at him and his plastic face tightened, and he watched me narrowly. "Kill her. It might as well be now. You were planning to kill her from the minute you walked us out of that office. I was already slated to die, wasn't I, Sid? How long? From the first?"

"What difference it make? You fly this thing. I tell you this. I can fly this plane. I don't need you."

"No. You're bluffing again. You can fly it. But just barely. They're coming after us—and you think I'm going to lose 'em for you."

"If you're smart you will."

"Yeah. But I'm not smart. If I was smart I'd have known you never intended splitting a hundred grand when you could take it all."

"Just shut up."

"Sure. And there's something else I'd have known if I had been smart. This whole job was for kicks. Your kicks. And that takes a killing doesn't it? Somebody at that bank. The constable—or me."

"I don't have to listen to you. You want it now?"

"Sure. Why not? You think I got some insane need to stick around and see what happens to you—or her?" I waited, watching him. I could look into his eyes, but they were flat now, something had gone out of them. "Come on, Coates. Get your kicks. Kill me, Coates. Come on, you strange-looking bastard. You going to kill me? Do it now. Get your kicks."

129

I raged at him, watching him sweat. He twitched, stirring, and then, suddenly making a strangled noise in his throat, he lifted the gun away from Judy's spine. I reacted with him, making one fluid motion of it. I sent the plane abruptly up and over so the whole thing shook and wailed. Judy didn't make a sound, but Coates screamed, toppling off balance. I fought the controls with one hand, bringing the plane around and level, and with the other I brought the wrench up from the floor, over my head and down into Coates' face. He didn't flinch. He took it, across the nose, across the forehead. The sound of metal crushing bone was sickening. I heard the roar of the gun and then the impact drove me hard against the door of the plane.

I brought the wrench down again. I could not see Coates. I couldn't hear him and I couldn't feel anything. But after what seemed an eternity, I heard Judy yelling at me and my eyes cleared and the earth was spinning and whirling upward toward us.

"Buz," she cried. "Oh, Buz, you're hurt."

I shook my head, trying to clear the red mist that fogged my vision. I worked the controls, watching the earth until it flattened out and the little plane went into a long even glide. It took everything I had ever learned to put the Cessna back to earth. We went down swiftly, but it all seemed to be happening very slowly. It took an eternity and then the wheels touched down and I laughed because we were nowhere near a runway. When I laughed, I tasted blood. I lifted my head and stared across the field. The police cars were racing toward us. I was thinking: they got me. The ground bastards got me. I glanced at Coates, flopped back, unconscious, his face bloody, but somehow looking no more outlandish than usual. He was the ground bastard who really pulled me down and showed me I was no better than be was. I didn't move. Finally the plane rolled to a stop and I cut the engine.

I said, "Judy, why don't you get out of here?"

"Oh, Buz."

"Go on. Get to hell out of here."

"I love you, Buz. I'll always love you."

"Get out."

She smiled, a twisted little smile full of tears. She leaned over and kissed my cheek, very gently. At least, I hardly felt it.

"All right, Buz. All right, darling."

She went away, opened the door, and was gone.

I didn't move. In the interminable distance, I saw the police cars racing across the field toward me. I tried to laugh, but I couldn't. They always won in the end, didn't they?

From far away I heard the scream of a siren, and I smiled to myself, thinking, I'll have to tell Greenie that I can't make that job in South America. I can never go down there as his equal now. . . .

But then I put the whole thing out of my mind. After all, you can't have everything. Can you?

BLACK LIZARD BOOKS